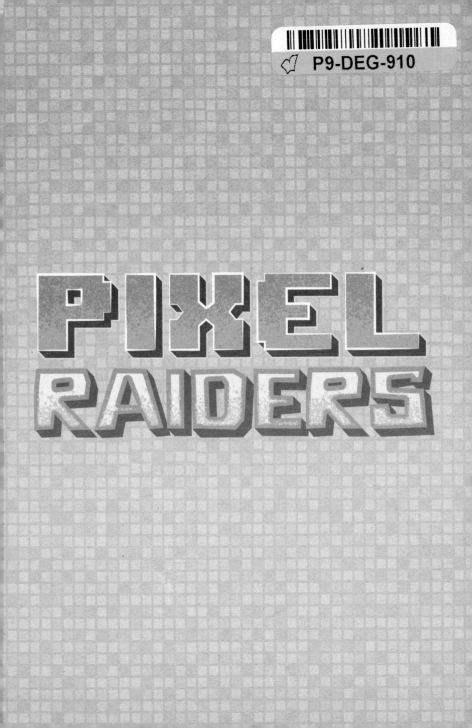

PIXEL RAIDERS

Dedicated to my friend Adam Chant, for his passionate advice on great books, and our shared love of science fiction. —**S.O.**

For my two wonderful nieces, Chloe and Leela. I hope this feeds your unquenchable sense of adventure. —**S.B.**

For Rose, my fiery little "Norbert." —**C.K.**

All rights reserved. Published by Scholastic Inc., *Publishers since 1920*, 557 Broadway, New York, NY 10012. SCHOLASTIC and associated logos are trademarks and/or registered trademarks of Scholastic Inc. This edition published under license from Scholastic Australia Pty Limited. First published by Scholastic Australia Pty Limited in 2016.

The publisher does not have any control over and does not assume any responsibility for author or third-party websites or their content.

This book is a work of fiction. Names, characters, places, and incidents are either the product of the author's imagination or are used fictitiously, and any resemblance to actual persons, living or dead, business establishments, events, or locales is entirely coincidental.

ISBN 978-1-338-16119-9

10 9 8 7 6 5 4 3 2   18 19 20 21 22

Printed in the U.S.A   40
First printing 2018
Book design by Baily Crawford

PIXEL RAIDERS

DRAGON LAND

BY STEPHANIE BENDIXSEN +
STEVEN O'DONNELL

ILLUSTRATED BY CHRIS KENNETT

SCHOLASTIC INC.

THE STORY SO FAR...

Ripley and Mei Lin were the best gamers in the school. But they failed their once-in-a-lifetime chance to become BETA testers of the latest unreleased game by mega blockbuster game developer INREAL GAMES.

So, imagine their surprise when a mysterious package from INREAL arrived at their school soon after. Inside the box was a special virtual reality device. Then something strange happened when Rip and Mei booted the game up: They were pulled from the real world into the video game itself.

They spent the last few days building, crafting, digging, and battling monsters in a blocky world of survival, **DIG WORLD**. They discovered what was in store if they did not survive when their schoolmate Angela was overcome by monsters and eventually became one herself.

It was then they really knew they were trapped.

They made it through **DIG WORLD** just in time, with the help of a giant crab wearing a monocle, and a powerful wizard named George. But they were not sent home as they had expected. Instead, they fell, tumbling through the sky until they landed on the back of a dragon.

We find them there now, aloft on the dragon, desperately clinging on, while a fierce battle is about to begin . . .

INTO THE FIRE

"**R**EMEMBER OUR ORDERS! FLY TRUE, STRIKE FAST, LIVE LONG!" the huge dragon bellowed. The powerful beast was soaring through the air so fast, its smooth green scales were hard for Rip and Mei to grip.

The nearby dragons flew in a V formation behind them, and Rip realized they were getting ready to attack. "Mei! I think this is a dragon battle!" he yelled.

"Yeah, I kind of guessed that the hundreds of dragons flying RIGHT NEXT TO US were getting ready to fight!" Mei shouted, still clinging tightly to the dragon's neck, which was quite warm and seemed to be getting hotter.

Rip was holding on to the dragon behind Mei, but could barely hear what she said. The roar of the wind and the *FWAP FWAP FWAP* of the huge beast's wings was deafening.

"It's like we're in the opening scene to an epic role-playing fantasy game!" Rip yelled excitedly at the top of his lungs. "We've entered another game or level or something!"

"Hey, Rip, let's talk about that later . . . we have to get off this thing or we might, you know, die!" Mei called back as a bug flew into her mouth, causing her to cough and splutter.

Then, without warning, the dragon corkscrewed downward, nearly throwing Rip and Mei off.

Rip vomited.

"GROSS!" Mei grimaced.

"Oops, sorry."

"HUUUUUUUMAN!" A deep voice rumbled like thunder, right next to Mei's head. It was another green dragon, keeping pace alongside them and staring right at Mei. The misshapen fangs in its mouth were long and sharp, and the eyes were red like fire. Mei could smell its horrible fishy breath. This was not like the blocky creatures they had encountered in the last game. This dragon looked much scarier.

"FREY!" the dragon called out. "THERE IS A HUMAN ON YOU!"

"WHAT? GET IT OFF!"

Frey, the dragon Rip and Mei were clinging

to, sounded horrified. She swung her head back and forth, trying to see them. As she did, Rip slipped and was spun around Frey's neck. He vomited ... again.

"GET IT OFF! GET IT OFF! EWW!" Frey yelled.

"I DON'T WANT TO TOUCH IT! AHHH! THERE'S ANOTHER ONE AROUND YOUR NECK TOO! AHHHHHH!" The other dragon sounded a little panicked.

Frey broke away from the formation of dragons, diving and spinning, trying to shake off Rip and Mei.

"Don't let go, Rip!" said Mei, glancing at her full health on her digital wristband. "If we fall here, we might not survive!"

Rip clung on even tighter, but at the sound of Mei's voice, Frey's flying became more

erratic.
She started
doing barrel
rolls, clearly
desperate to
shake them off.

"Can't we ...
uh ... talk
about this ...
uh!" Rip tried
to reason with
Frey, as they
were flung left and
right, up and down. "You can
just let us off ... gently, you know!"

"DON'T YOU DARE SPEAK TO ME, VILE
HUMAN!" Frey growled with fury.

"I don't think he likes us!" Rip yelled to Mei.

"AND I AM NOT A HE!" Frey added.

"Sorry!" Rip said. "I'm new to dragons!
And ... uh ... *BURP* ... flying! Uh-oh, I think
I'm gonna ..."

"NOOOO! YUCK!" Frey bellowed and dived straight down. She headed for a thick, dark part of a forest below. Rip and Mei had totally lost visuals on the dragon army, but could hear what sounded like lightning storms and explosions off in the distance.

"TIME FOR A BATH, DIRTY HUMANS!" Frey roared.

SPLASH!

BORN TO FLY

Mei's lungs burned as she held her breath beneath the water, desperately trying to wriggle free of the tangle of weeds that had wrapped themselves around her ankle. She needed air. *Right now.*

With a final, determined thrash of her foot, the plants released their grip and she launched herself toward the surface, bursting into the open air and gratefully filling her lungs with loud gulps. Her waterlogged backpack was seriously weighing her down, but she didn't dare leave it behind.

"MEI!" Rip was swimming madly toward her, a relieved expression on his face. "You're OK!"

Mei nodded and wiped slick, slimy swamp water from her face as she felt around for ground shallow enough to stand on.

"Well, this is just great," she grumbled. "It's practically the first rule of fantasy games: Avoid swamps at all costs. And where do we end up?"

Rip nodded in agreement. "I know. Swamps are dark. They're smelly. Full of germs and leeches. *And* you never know what else might be lurking beneath—"

As if on cue, the water in the swamp lake began to bubble. The color drained from Rip and Mei's faces as they quickly scrambled out of the water. It was clear that whatever was under there—it was big.

"ARRRGGHHHHH!" roared the dragon, launching herself out of the swamp, tangled in reeds and dripping slime. She made a few

struggling attempts to flap her wings but she only managed to twist herself into even more of a snarled mess as she flopped onto the muddy shore.

Rip took a tentative step toward Frey. "Um . . . do you need some help?"

"NO HELP!" the dragon bellowed.

Rip nodded. "Right. Well . . . you see, Frey, we could probably find a way to cut through those weeds and—"

"NO HELP!" Frey bellowed again, attempting to make her point even clearer by expelling a modest, burning cloud of fire in their direction. Fortunately for Rip and Mei, it seemed the dragon's ability to create huge, searing fireballs had been diminished somehow.

"HEY!" Rip and Mei cried out together, stumbling backward away from the puff of flame.

"We were just trying to help," Mei said sourly.

"No help," Frey said one last time, a little more gently. She snorted a soft cloud of smoke and shuffled off into the trees, wings flexing against the constraints of the mud and weeds that covered her.

"What a horrible creature," said Mei.

Rip nodded, but continued to stare into the twisted forest where Frey had gone. "You have to admit, flying on a dragon was kind of fun," he said sheepishly. "Apart from the fact we could've died."

A smile crept across Mei's face. "Yeah. It really was. I just ... I thought dragons would be ... different."

"Different how?"

Mei shrugged. "I dunno. Never mind. Let's get going. This seems like a brand-new world, so we're going to have to figure out the rules."

Rip nodded in agreement. "At least that bit

of flame dried us off a little. Oh, hey!" He brightened. "Looks like I'm still on full health!"

Mei checked her wristband and saw three full hearts displayed. "Me too! The swamp goo must have broken our fall enough not to knock off any health."

"You look great, by the way," Rip said with a laugh, slinging a glob of slime at Mei's already slimy face.

Mei giggled. "Yeah, you too, slime-o. Maybe it'll work in our favor. Like camoflage!"

"Pee-ew! It's pretty stinky camoflage," Rip said, getting a whiff of his own odor.

They laughed again. It felt good to laugh.

Then their laughter was interrupted by a bellowing sound coming from deeper in the swamp forest.

"That sounded like Frey," Rip said.

Mei stared nervously into the trees. "Rip, we tried to help her. She doesn't want anything to do with us. We should get out of here!"

Rip shook his head. "She sounded like she's in pain or something."

Another bellow—this time more of a howl— rang out into the air.

Mei sighed. "Fine. What weapons do we have?"

Rip checked his pack. "I have some of the block weapons from the previous game . . . but they seem kind of inferior for a world like this."

"Better than nothing though, right?" Mei said. "We'll upgrade our gear as soon as we get the chance."

Rip hoisted his pixelated bow out of his

magical inventory pack, along with a handful of arrows.

Mei looked through her own inventory until she found an axe—better suited to cutting wood, but it would have to do.

Together, they trudged warily into the forest. Clouds of green, smelly gas lingered around their feet as they squelched through the mud. Mei pulled her T-shirt up over her nose and mouth in an attempt to filter out the stench.

"It's like the fart flowers all over again," she moaned. "I love the idea of virtual reality games—ones you don't get stuck in, that is— but do they have to be so stinky?!"

"Shhh, Mei . . ." Rip stopped, staring ahead. "There. By that cave."

Mei turned and saw Frey, desperately trying to fly but still tangled in swamp weeds. In front of her, wildly swinging an impressive- looking sword, was a knight dressed in full black-plate armor. A plume of bright red

feathers crested a helmet and visor.

With impressive force, the knight launched forward and sliced at Frey's neck. Her tough scales protected her from the glancing blow—but next time she might not be so lucky.

Mei gasped. "Rip . . ."

Rip nodded. "I know."

They were both annoyed at what had happened with Frey, but neither of them wanted to watch any creature be attacked while unable to defend itself.

They ran toward the fight.

The knight leapt at Frey again. Only this time, she countered with a swipe of her

mighty clawed arm—restricted though it was with caked mud and vines. The blow glanced off the knight's head, knocking the plumed helmet to the ground.

Rip and Mei stopped dead in their tracks.

"BRAYDEN?" they both said at once.

Brayden looked up at them, surprised. "Hey, what's up, NOOBS!" He grinned. "Here to watch me slay this beast like a pro?"

Mei still remembered the way Brayden had taunted her at the INREAL GAMES excursion after purposely tripping her up. She opened her mouth to give him a piece of her mind—but found herself unable to speak. Her mouth gaped like a fish.

Brayden snorted. "What are you NOOBS even doing here?! You guys failed like a bunch of mega losers!" His laughter broadened into an irritating cackle.

Mei's cheeks burned with embarrassment and anger. But Brayden didn't wait for a reply. Sword in hand, he turned his attention back to the fight, moving toward Frey, who was now lying down and breathing heavily, exhausted. She had given up.

Brayden lifted his sword high above his head, ready to land the final blow.

"YO!" Rip yelled, nocking an arrow into his pixel bow. "How's this for NOOBERY?!"

He released the arrow. Mei sprinted toward Brayden.

"Argh, NO!" Brayden scowled as Mei slid past, disarming him. "I had this! I need the

materials from this thing to craft dragon scale armor. It's, like, top tier—the best you can get in the game!"

Holding the sword she had skillfully seized from Brayden, Mei finally found her voice. "Listen. Cool it, will you? Can't you see she's in pain?"

"So? It's just a game. Who cares?"

Rip and Mei exchanged glances. "Well . . . we're not so sure about that," Rip said slowly. "About this . . . just being a game, I mean."

Mei nodded solemnly. "We've seen some crazy stuff. We saw . . . Angela. She died in the game and . . . she . . . she turned into a spider."

Brayden scoffed, "Yeah, right."

"She's telling the truth. I saw it too." Rip's eyes were wide. "Plus, we tried to leave, and

we couldn't. Have you even tried removing your headset?"

Brayden looked between the two of them, clearly unnerved now. But then his expression darkened. He shook his head. "You guys are just trying to psych me out so YOU can get the dragon scale gear and finish this game first!" he sneered. "But you won't. Keep the sword—I know where I can get a better one anyway. Later, NOOBS."

Brayden started to run, heading farther into the forest. He paused and turned around to yell, "Hey, Mei Lin. Watch your step."

Mei's eyes stung and she swallowed. Why was he so horrible to her? And why could she never think of anything clever to say back to his dumb remarks?

"Don't worry about him," Rip said, patting her on the shoulder. "He's just a bully."

The two gamers turned their attention back to Frey. They got to work slicing through the weeds, and peeling clumps of swamp

slime from her once shiny emerald scales.
She was too tired to protest.

When the worst of the muck had been
removed, the dragon climbed to her feet and
gingerly flexed her wings—and winced. She
wouldn't be returning to the skies anytime
soon.

"Well, humans." She breathed a gravelly
sigh, with her usual plumes of smoke. "A fine
mess you've made of things! It would seem I
now owe you a debt."

Rip shook his head. "You don't owe us
anything. Really."

Frey's eyes glittered and she lowered her
enormous reptilian head until it was only
inches from Rip's and Mei's faces. "But you
are mistaken. When you saved my life, we
became magically bound."

Mei swallowed. "What do you mean?"

Frey rolled her eyes. "It's an ancient spell.
We're stuck with each other. From this
moment forth, where you go . . . I go. Which is

bad, because the two of you are stinky. And I mean stinky—even for humans!"

She snorted as if to demonstrate the offense to her nostrils.

"That can't be right," Rip said, aghast.

"Ah, but it is!" came a familiar voice from behind them.

DRAGON RIDERS

George was casually chewing what looked like a long turnip. "Dragon Riders!" he said, in between mouthfuls. "Welcome to DRAGON LAND! An epic medieval adventure! Word of your adventures so far has already spread throughout the land!" *CHOMP.* "It is good to see you again."

George was still dressed in the same long, flowing white robe he wore in **DIG WORLD**. He had the same tree-branch staff, with red veins twisting around the top. They pulsed slowly in the dim forest, giving off a little light, creating spooky, dancing

shadows among the trees around them.

CHOMP

The wizard tossed what was left of his turnip over his shoulder. "It appears you've already picked your first companion!" He eyed the dragon. "And what a companion, might I say!"

Frey snorted disapprovingly, black smoke puffing out of each of her nostrils directly over Rip and Mei. They both coughed heavily. Frey made a low grumbling noise that almost sounded like a laugh. She stepped toward George.

"I am no companion," Frey said proudly, but without malice. There was respect in her tone as she addressed George, almost as if she could recognize his power. "I am Frey the Devourer, Third Lieutenant Dragon of the Fire Enclave, and eighth in line for the throne of DragonLord Garonoth."

The mighty dragon bowed her head slightly to George, without breaking eye contact.

"A mighty pleasure to meet you, Frey the Devourer, Third Lieutenant Dragon of the Fire Enclave, and eighth in line for the throne of DragonLord Garonoth!" said the old wizard, and he did a half-bow, half-curtsy toward the dragon. "I am George."

George turned to Mei and Rip, his wrinkled face suddenly became far less comical, and he whispered cautiously, "Be careful with this one. She's magically bound to follow you for now, but know that is all that's stopping her from turning you both into toasted humans."

There was a rumble above them, and a crack of lightning. Rip and Mei hadn't noticed a storm had rolled in, and how dark it was getting.

"We should probably find shelter," Rip said.

"Also, George, we have a LOT of questions!" Mei added.

"Yeah, like why are we here?" Rip folded his arms and continued, "You ALSO said you were sending us home!"

"Technically, I said I would get you out of the world you were in. And that, I did!"

George smiled and, without warning, a cat fell on his head.

"Meep," it said, as it bounced off George's head and landed on the ground in front of him. The little creature blinked its eyes a couple of times. It looked confused, and then noticed Frey licking her big crusty dragon lips.

"Meeeeeep, meep, meep . . ." it squealed, running off into the forest.

"Looks like rain!" George said, and giggled as a few more small cats and a couple of puppies landed near them. Some got stuck in trees.

"Meep, meep . . ."

"Yelp, yelp, yelp . . ."

It actually was raining cats and dogs.

"Come with me, we have much to discuss!" George

27

beckoned. He turned around and began walking down a narrow muddy trail.

"Are we really not going to talk about the raining animals?" Rip asked, sidestepping a couple of pugs, who were rolling around in the dirt. He bent down to pat one on the belly. It licked his hands.

Mei smiled and resisted the urge to pick it up and kiss its little pug face.

"But first, we must traverse the Path of Never-Ending Darkness!" George said, ignoring Rip and throwing his arms dramatically into the air as he spoke. "Then all shall be revealed. WOooOOOooo!"

They walked for a long time, following the wizard down the twisting path. The forest became denser and denser the farther they traveled. George's staff bobbed about like a lone firefly in the darkness, giving off just enough light to see where they were going.

Mei occasionally looked back at the giant dragon begrudgingly stomping behind them. Frey's eyes were unblinking and fixed on the two gamers, and her brow stayed in a perpetual frown. And yet, she made very little noise for a beast so large. Mei didn't like that the dragon appeared to be tethered to them and not free to leave. But she was also glad it was on their side. The game was only just beginning, and who knew what challenges lay ahead.

Rip's thoughts were on gear. Specifically, Brayden's armor. It had looked amazing. Rip was a competitive gamer. No matter how hard he tried to not care what others had, if he saw someone online who had a better bow or hat than him, he *had* to have it.

Rip was just about to ask George how much farther they had to walk when the path opened into a small clearing and they stopped in front of a giant tree that stood in the middle. The trunk stretched far up into the sky, disappearing into the dense canopy above. It looked old. Much older than the rest of the forest.

There was a cracking noise, and two giant eyes and a wide mouth slowly formed in the wooden trunk.

The wood face spoke. "PAAAASSWOOOORD."

George scratched his head. "Oh . . . ah, I always forget this . . . Jelly top hats! That's it!"

The tree yawned widely, and George stepped inside. Rip and Mei gave each other

concerned looks, both hesitant to jump in the mouth of a giant tree.

George walked back out again. "Come on, you two! Don't be afraid of old Woody here!" he said, as he knocked his fist twice on the giant tree's face. "He's harmless, but you will need to leave your dragon outside! She's too big!"

George walked back in. He walked back out again. "You'll like this part! It's time to pick a class!"

He walked back in.

Rip and Mei shrugged and followed. The tree's mouth closed behind them.

Outside, Frey turned in a circle three times and finally curled up like a sleepy dog in front of the tree. She mumbled, "I'm not their dragon. I'm not anyone's dragon."

Frey closed her eyes and instantly started snoring so loudly the nearby trees shook with every breath.

YOU GOT CLASS

Stepping inside the tree took Rip and Mei into a space that was much larger than it looked from the outside. Instead of a hollow trunk, they found themselves in an enormous room with four elaborately gilded mirrors standing before them. The mirrors all hummed softly, each one glowing brightly with a different colored light.

"Well . . . ?" George said, exasperated. "Don't just stand there like a couple of swamp toads.

Each mirror represents the four classes: ranger, tank, healer, and mage. So, go on ... pick a class!"

He did a little jig on the spot and clapped excitedly.

Rip and Mei glanced at each other.

Then Rip stepped up to the first mirror, which glowed a vivid green, and examined his reflection.

In the green light, he felt an immediate connection to the forest. He saw himself dressed head-to-toe in fine tanned leather armor. On his back was a quiver packed full of arrows, each fletched with striped turkey feathers. Best of all, however, was the bow. It was a thing of beauty—crafted from one single piece of wood, with a curling inscription in a language he didn't recognize.

"Walk softly, strike true," George translated, in a hushed, reverential tone. "How do you like yourself, Ranger Rip?"

Rip was at a complete loss for words. He

gazed at his reflection, dumbfounded. He loved the ranger class. Quick and stealthy, rangers dealt smaller amounts of damage in quick succession—and often crept into fights unnoticed. "I . . . I never knew I could look so . . ."

"So . . . what?" George urged.

"So EPIC!" Rip grinned broadly. "Seriously, I look AWESOME!"

George giggled. "Huzzah! So, you accept this role?"

"Yes, I do!" Rip shivered as his skin tingled for a moment. And when he looked down, his

real-life self now matched his reflection. He noted that his backpack had vanished, but all his items could be accessed by simply reaching into his pockets. "Oh, Mei . . . you've got to try this!" Rip spun around and

whooped happily. "What class are you going to pick?"

Mei was standing in front of the red mirror, gazing at a reflection of herself dressed in the shining plate armor of a knight. "I think ... I am a knight."

She frowned, watching as her reflected image made measured strikes with a sword. This must have been the class Brayden had chosen.

"The tank class, a fine choice!" George nodded approvingly. "As a knight, you'll be first into the fray. Tanks are the damage absorbers!"

"Agro-puller!" Rip chimed in. "You are pretty great with a sword, Mei."

Mei chewed her lip thoughtfully. "I'm just not sure. It lacks ... finesse. Can I choose another one?"

George made a sweeping gesture toward the remaining two mirrors, his arm getting tangled in his long, white beard in the

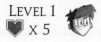

process. "Dang-dingle-doodly-poop!" he muttered, busying himself with the mess. Mei stepped away from the red mirror to the next one, which was pulsating a mysterious blue.

This time in the reflective glass, Mei saw herself swathed in an elaborate robe of purple and blue, embroidered with detailed curling patterns in silver thread. The robe fell right down to the floor at the back—but was short in the front for ease of movement, revealing a pair of dark-blue trousers and fine black boots underneath. A large, dusty spell book rested in her left hand and in her right, a crackling ball of blue light hovered at her fingertips.

Mei took a sharp, inward breath.

"Whoa . . ." Rip was equally impressed. "You look . . ."

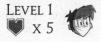
"Powerful," Mei finished for him, her lips curling into a smile. The mage class was useful in similar ways to the ranger—being able to make strong attacks from a distance. But instead of wielding a weapon, they used spells and magic. "I choose this one."

George, who had finally managed to free himself from his own beard, gazed up at her and nodded. "Yes, yes. This fits you perfectly, I agree." He snapped his fingers and Mei felt a light fizz across her skin as the impressive outfit appeared on her body—just as it was in the mirror. "Fight well, Mage Mei."

"So . . . wait. This means we have no knight!" Rip said, his shoulders sagging. "We can't have an adventuring party with just a ranger and a mage. Who's going to act as the tank and take the damage?"

Mei's brow furrowed. "I guess I still could?"

Rip snorted, gesturing to her cloth robe. "Uh, not in that outfit you couldn't."

"Well, there's got to be a shield spell in here

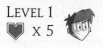

somewhere," Mei argued, rifling through the pages of her newly acquired spell book.

"AHEM"—George cleared his throat, a sound that went on and on like a car failing to start—"AHEMAHEMAHEMAHEM!" He looked from one adventurer to the other. "But you already have someone to be your knight."

Mei looked confused. "I hope you don't mean Brayden because he is NOT on our side."

"No, no, no," George shook his head, exasperated again. "You have Frey! Frey is your knight, obviously! She's strong, has her own natural built-in armor, and at her size she will certainly 'pull aggression' the moment you three enter a fight."

Rip's eyebrows shot up. "I guess it will be kind of handy having a dragon in our group!"

Mei nodded in agreement.

"Yes, what you don't have, unfortunately, is a healer." George motioned to the final mirror, which glowed a soft yellow-gold. "But

there's nothing we can really do about that. Now! It's time to HEAD OFF!"

George skipped toward the tree-door, which opened wide, revealing Frey's great, sleeping head outside.

Frey yawned and blinked, then gazed up at them. "Well, you two have certainly had a transformation."

Rip and Mei stepped proudly out into the forest, displaying their new gear.

"Yeah. We picked our classes." Rip grinned. "You're the knight."

Frey snorted a short puff of smoke. "Figures. I hope you don't expect me to wave a sword around."

Mei stifled a giggle. "Wait," she said, turning back to George. "What's our quest? Like . . . our objective? You don't just run randomly out into a fantasy world without some sort of quest!"

All eyes turned to George, who stroked his beard thoughtfully. "Indeed, indeed. Right you are, young Mage." He launched into a more heraldic speaking voice. "There will be many quests that you must undertake on this journey. Some great. Some small. But at the end of this journey you MUST have retrieved a single, sacred item in order to leave this place..." He paused for dramatic effect. "You must obtain... ThE ETHERSTONE."

Frey coughed and began to splutter. Rip and Mei looked up at her worryingly.

"What's... the Etherstone?" Rip asked, turning his attention back to George. "Can it get us home?"

"Indeed it can!" replied George with a crooked smile, wagging his finger playfully.

"How?" Rip asked "Tell us!"

"Little travelers, that kind of reward requires a price. Bring me the stone, and I'll give you advice." George put his hands on his hips and smiled. "Hey, that rhymed!"

POOF

There was a bright flash of light and a puff of smoke, and George was gone. In his place was a tiny kitten. "Mew!" it said, then scampered off into the forest, presumably to join the other kittens and puppies from before. Rip shook his head, baffled.

Frey had managed to compose herself, but had a grim expression on her reptilian face. "The Etherstone is a very powerful and ancient artifact," she explained. "It is known to all who live in this land."

We don't. That is . . . we *can't.*

Right. So how do we get it?

FIRST QUEST FIRST

"It's on the what now?" Rip asked Frey.

The three adventurers had begun to walk along the winding path, through the dark forest. Rip and Mei listened closely as Frey explained the perils of their quest.

"The stone you seek is on the crown of the mighty DragonLord Garonoth."

"All right, where is this DragonLord?" Rip said, while tightening the buckles on his new leather wrist guards. "Let's go get it!"

"BWAAAHAHAHAHA!" Frey chortled, bellowing foul-smelling smoke with each snort. "You do not simply 'go get' the DragonLord's crown."

"Why not?" asked Mei, doing her best to look tough in front of Frey. "I think you'll find

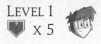

that we have a lot of experience in this kind of thing."

"Oh, do you, human?" Frey said, with a hint of humor in her deep, gravelly voice. "From the look of you both, I'd say you were probably Level 1. Level 2 at best. How many hearts do you have?"

Rip and Mei looked at their wristbands and noticed that the digital display had changed in appearance.

"Mine says Level 1 and I have five hearts," Mei said.

"Me too," said Rip.

Frey smiled. "Ha! Level 1! DragonLord Garonoth is Level 10 and has fifty hearts. I doubt you'd survive even one swipe of the DragonLord's tail."

Rip and Mei looked at each other, a little defeated. Role-playing games always had tough boss fights. If defeating Garonoth and obtaining the stone from his crown was their final goal in this game, it made sense they

wouldn't be able to do it right away.

"No one has ever defeated Garonoth," Frey continued. "Many have tried. All have failed."

"So what do we do?" Mei asked Frey.

"You both seem to be under the impression I wish to help you," Frey said, a frown forming on her scaly face. "I am bound to you, and will fight beside you. This is DRAGONLAW. But I am not your friend. I am not going to tell you how to defeat the leader of my clan."

Frey stomped off the path to a nearby tree and began scratching her neck along the trunk.

"OK, let's put the brakes on for a moment," Mei said. "To escape this world, we need the stone from this DragonLord's crown. Right?"

"Right. I think," Rip replied. For a moment, he'd forgotten they were trapped in a video game. It was like the more they played, the further away the real world felt, and the less he thought about it.

"So," Mei continued, "we need to get tough enough for the final fight. These kinds of

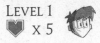 
games are always quite long and focus on the steady progression of difficulty and stats. So to get tough enough, we need to grind out some side quests."

"Right!" Rip said. "So where do we find those?"

At that very moment, a small dwarf appeared on the path ahead, riding a very small donkey, which looked like it was struggling with the load. The stocky dwarf was dressed in mud-stained overalls and had a pitchfork in one hand. Around his head buzzed several firebugs. The dwarf also had a giant yellow exclamation mark above his head, which moved and bobbed along with him.

"Well met, Dragon Riders!" he said, slapping his face where a firebug landed on it. The squished little bug coughed a tiny puff of fire, before disappearing in a small shower of pixels.

"Er . . . hi," said Rip.

"How about dis dragon war, eh? Tearin' up me farm, dey are! Eatin' all me sheep and burnin' me crops! I wish something could be done to make 'em all get along, like in de olden days!" The farmer pulled out a letter and handed it to Mei. "Here, take dis letter to town for me, will ya? Tell the soldiers to send help!"

Mei took the letter. As she did, the exclamation mark disappeared from above the dwarf's head in a puff of yellow sparkles.

"Thanks, Dragon Riders! There'll be a nice reward in it for you! Oh, and 'ere's a map in case ya get lost!" The farmer handed another piece of paper to Rip. "Farewell, Dragon Riders! Watch out for bandits, they favor newcomers to these trails!"

The dwarf kicked his heels into the donkey, who grunted with annoyance as it continued slowly along the trail.

"Is our first quest really going to be a letter delivery?" Rip asked Mei. "That's so

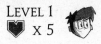

boring. I want to test out this new bow!" Rip was tugging at the string of his bow and firing pretend shots into the distance.

Mei was also keen to test out her spell book. "Maybe we can find some more quests in town."

"Come on, Frey!" Rip yelled as he started walking, holding out the map in one hand and swatting away one of the lurking firebugs with the other. "We need to go, uh, this way! Along the Path of Never-Ending ... *Bandits*?" Rip rolled his eyes. "Wow, I wonder what's going to happen on the Path of Never-Ending Bandits," he said sarcastically.

FIREBUG DATA MISSION #17060402
TARGETS ACQUIRED

ALERT! INCOMING! EVASIVE MANEUVERS!
Skew left, 42°. Angle body right.
Spin 30% Dive. Pull up.

The firebug had only basic instructions. It buzzed around the ranger's head.

The firebug was now out of range. It allowed itself a moment to hover and observe. It watched the dwarf and the donkey. It watched the mage. It watched the ranger. It watched the dragon. It stored their details.

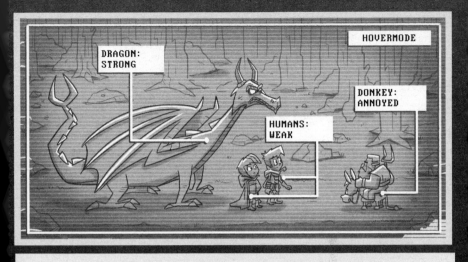

10% power. HOVERMODE. Observe. Report.
Simple instructions. Limited memory.
The humans are weak. STORED. The dragon
is strong. STORED. The donkey is annoyed.
Not important. DELETED. Something about
the crown. STORED. A stone of power.
STORED.
FLAGGED IMPORTANT FOR THE FIRELORD.

GO FETCH

As they made their way farther into the forest, Frey suddenly moaned. "I can't go that way, I'm too big."

Rip rolled his eyes, annoyed. "Of course you can. Just put one foot in front of the other, silly."

Mei examined the path ahead. Low hanging branches and thick bushes made the path even narrower. "She may have a point, Rip. The forest just gets more and more dense."

"Besides," Frey grumbled, "I'm tired. I'm used to flying—I've never had to walk this much before. I wish my wings would heal."

"Another reason a healer would be useful." Mei sighed. Then she had a thought. "Wait— what if . . ." She began rifling through her spell

book, her two companions watching on curiously. "Aha! I've got it." Mei planted her feet firmly in the soil and raised her right hand. "I'm a little new to this, so, uh . . . I'm sorry if this goes wrong."

Frey blinked.

Mei began murmuring in a strange, magical language Rip had never heard before. The blue ball of light sprung to life in her fingers, and with a crackle it zapped angrily toward the dragon. There was a sudden flash, and the beast was gone.

Rip stared in stunned silence.

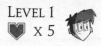

"Wh—where did she go?!"

"Ahem!" A loud squeak could be heard below them. Frey hadn't gone anywhere. But she was now very, very tiny. "I hope this isn't permanent!" the shrunken dragon yelped, shocked and angry.

Mei smiled in relief. "Nope. There's another incantation right here to reverse it." Mei pointed to the book. "But at least now you are more portable!" She giggled.

Mei lifted the tiny, cranky dragon—who was now no greater in size than a mouse—and tucked her safely into one of the pockets in her robe.

"You gonna be OK in there?" Mei asked, peering into the pocket carefully.

But Frey ignored her, stomped around in a circle, curled up, and went to sleep. Her dragon snores could still be heard, despite her size.

"She sure does sleep a lot," Rip said dryly. "Some battle companion."

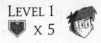

The forest path was dark but beautiful. Unusual, colorful plant life sprung up amid the gnarled and twisted trees that lined their way. A rustle in the bushes revealed a strange, long-eared rodent, which scampered across the forest floor in front of them before disappearing into bushes on the other side.

"Everything here is so weird . . ." Rip mused, snatching a low-hanging fruit from a nearby tree as he walked. It was oval, slightly transparent, and pulsated a soft orange color. "Hey—dare me to eat this?"

Mei shrugged. "I guess. Oddly enough, I'm not at all hungry."

"Neither am I," Rip realized. "I guess because this isn't a survival game, we don't have to keep track of our hunger."

"Food is handy to restore health and stuff though," Mei pointed out. "Maybe you should try it."

Needing no further encouragement, Rip took a hearty bite of the unknown fruit. A brilliant burst of flavors exploded into his mouth all at once. First the tang of something intensely sweet that reminded him of  sorbet. Then a kind of softness, like marshmallow. Lastly, a dancing firework of peppermint sparkled across his tongue. Rip's eyes grew wide.

"Oh . . . oh wow. WOW. Mei, you have got to try this!" He chewed enthusiastically.

"Uh, Ripley . . ." Mei was staring at him, her mouth hanging open. "You're kind of glowing."

Rip looked down at himself. "Huh?" Sure enough, his skin had taken on a soft, orange glow. "Oh yeah."

"Do you feel OK?"

"I feel fine." Rip stretched and tossed what

was left of the fruit into the bushes. "I feel better than fine, actually."

Mei's eyes narrowed. "What do you mean, 'better than fine'? Do you mean...stronger? Tougher?"

Mei punched him in the arm suddenly.

"HEY!" Rip exclaimed. "Why'd you—hey, I didn't even feel that. Do it again. Maybe a bit harder."

Mei hesitated. "Are you sure? I don't want to hurt you."

Rip nodded. Mei slogged him in the arm—a lot harder this time. Rip shook his head. "Didn't feel a thing. I know I'm wearing armor, but I should have felt something, right?"

Mei smiled. "I think you've got a buff!"

Rip gasped, realizing what she meant. "Of course. From that fruit! I must be like... invincible now or something!"

"Well, let's not go crazy. You may just be a little stronger than usual. And it may not last that long either, or you'd be over-powered."

"True," Rip agreed. "We should grab more of that fruit!"

They both eagerly studied the fruit tree but could only find one fruit left, hanging daintily from a curling twig. Mei plucked it carefully from the branch, and tucked it safely into one of the leather pouches on her mage's belt.

"Best save it for when we really need it," Mei said. She nudged Rip playfully and added, "You'd be terrible in a game of hide-and-seek right now."

They both laughed, and Ripley did a little dance as his glowing skin lit their way through the shadowy forest.

After a while, the path began to widen and open out, revealing a small valley, at the bottom of which lay a beautiful town surrounded by a stone wall. Glad to leave the dark canopy of the forest, Rip and Mei stepped out into the sunlight.

"I bet that's where we're supposed to deliver the letter," Rip said, cheerful to have the warmth of light on his face now that his "fruit buff" had worn off.

Mei took the letter out of her robe pocket. "We're probably going to get a pretty good reward for handing this in, so we'll have to keep it safe."

"Actually, you can give that to me, Dragon Riders," came a gruff voice from the edge of the trees. "And we'll see about this reward."

ACTIONS AND CONSEQUENCES

There were three bandits in total.

A tall, skinny woman leaned against a tree. She was chewing a long piece of grass, grinning a nasty smile, like she was getting ready to enjoy whatever was coming next. A short, fat man was jumping up and down. He had the face of a naughty child, and was giggling to himself. And a tough-looking man wearing light chain mail stood with a whip by his side. He had a calm but menacing face.

He cracked the whip before speaking. "I said, you can give that to me."

"And why would we do that?" said Mei defiantly. She was speaking in a tone that radiated strength.

Rip wasn't so confident. "Yeah ... um ... why

58

would we want to do that? It's our quest and
our reward."

The bandit with the whip seemed to be the
leader of the group. He stepped closer,
staring Rip down.

Rip continued, "I mean, we don't want any
trouble or anything, so, um ... leave us alone
or else ... or else we'll ..."

"You'll what?" the lead bandit said, poking
Rip in the chest with a dirty finger. "Hit me
with your little bow and arrow? HAR, HAR,
HAR." His tone became low and cold. "Fact of
the matter is, young'un, we own this road
into town. And if you want to pass, you need
to pay the toll."

"Hehuheuhehuh, dah toll," said the short,

fat bandit stupidly.

The skinny one was a little scarier. She stepped closer and started expertly spinning a rusty sword so fast that it became a blur.

Mei raised an eyebrow, impressed by the bandit's swordplay skills.

"Two gold pieces to pass," said the leader, moving his face even closer to Rip's, so their noses were almost touching. Rip could smell his foul breath.

"We haven't got any money," said Mei, stepping in closer to get the leader's attention. He shifted his eyes to her, but he didn't move. "So you might as well let us go; we have nothing for you," said Mei casually.

The leader stepped back and Rip sucked in a huge breath of fresh air.

"Well, the way I see it, mah dear, is that you two rascals 'ere have three choices," the bandit said, dragging the whip behind him as he paced in front of them. "Choice one: Pay us two pieces of gold. Choice two: Give us

that there letter in your hands."

"And choice three?" Rip said, already knowing the answer.

. "Well, choice three will be an interesting one, won't it, boy?" The bandit stopped, pulled out his whip, and gave it another almighty crack, forcing Rip to duck to avoid it hitting his face.

"Hey!" Rip said.

The other two bandits moved up next to their leader's side.

"I like choice three," the skinny bandit said as she scraped her sword along the dirt. "That's my favorite."

The fat one giggled, flipping a coin in one hand.

Rip turned to Mei and whispered, "You should just give them the letter and we can be on our way. There's bound to be more quests in town."

"They don't look so tough," Mei whispered back, stuffing the letter into her pocket.

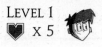

"Plus, I have a dragon in my pocket if things get rough. We need the experience too. If we take them out, we might even level up!"

"I think this is a classic choice/consequence sequence," Rip said. "They're giving us three options, so there will probably be a different outcome each way. We should choose carefully."

"It's our first quest, Rip! Plus, they'll just harass whoever else comes down this path. We'll be doing a good deed, and I think our reputation status matters here. Everyone seems to know us as 'Dragon Riders' already, so that's good. If we do this, the people of this land might like us more and give us more quests. And that can help us level up."

Rip frowned, thinking hard. "We haven't really practiced with our classes yet, though. I just think we . . ."

Mei flipped open her spell book and read out a series of strange words. A ball of ice instantly formed in her hands, and she threw

it at the skinny bandit.

The ice ball hit Mei's target, freezing the skinny bandit's legs. The leader then sprang into action, charging toward Rip and flicking the whip at him.

But Mei wasn't paying attention. She was conjuring her next spell. With a flick of her arm, she sent a green ball of goo sailing through the air toward the skinny bandit, who had just broken free of her leg cast of ice by bashing at it with her sword.

"Bull's-eye! That's called a snotterball," Mei boasted. "Yeah . . . it's made of snot."

The skinny bandit, still struggling with the goo, kicked the rusty sword at her feet toward Mei, knocking her over. Mei's wristband beeped. She was now down to four hearts too.

Rip was panicking. The leader was pulling him closer and closer, one hand at a time dragging in the whip.

"Come 'ere, you!" the leader said. "It's time to pay the toll!"

"Dah toll! Dah toll! Hurhurhur!" said the fat bandit, still giggling to himself.

Rip closed his eyes and pushed out hard, trying to break free.

The whip fell to the ground in a heap, and

BINK!

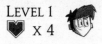 

Rip was gone. Vanished. The leader was dumbfounded.

BINK

Rip reappeared in a puff of gray smoke, a few steps behind the lead bandit.

"I shadowstepped!" he said, looking down, now free of the whip. Disappearing and reappearing behind an enemy was a classic teleport move for sneaky classes.

Level 2 flashed up on Rip's wristband. They'd leveled up!

Before the leader could figure out what had just happened, Rip reached into his quiver, grabbed the first arrow he could feel, and loaded it into his bow. It was a bolas arrow— two rocks separated by a short bit of rope, with an arrow on the end to guide it. Perfect.

BINK!

In one swift movement, Rip aimed and fired it at the leader's legs. The rocks

spun around his feet, tying them up and knocking him to the ground. The bandit shattered into a thousand tiny square pixels.

The skinny bandit finally cleared the goo from her eyes and ran full speed at Mei.

Mei was back on her feet, and reading a complicated string of words from her spell book. A giant ball of ice formed above her head, spinning and howling around a center of green goo. "Let's see what happens when you mix snot with ice."

Mei waved her arms and the snot-ice ball hurtled through the air, crashing into the skinny bandit in an explosion of ice and snot. Bits of frozen goo showered down from the sky and splashed into the puddle of pixels and gunk where the skinny bandit used to exist. It was almost beautiful, Mei thought.

Rip and Mei both turned to face the short, fat bandit. He wasn't laughing anymore. He was looking decidedly gray. He ran.

HELLO, DRAGON RIDERS

"Quest City," Mei read from the sign above two very large wooden gates. "That's the best name they could come up with?"

Rip shrugged. "At least we know we're in the right place!"

The two had made their way to the city and had hidden in the outskirts until dusk—just in case the third bandit came back to look for them. Unfortunately, Rip and Mei arrived quite late to the main gates, which now looked closed for the night.

Torches lit up the high city walls, which stretched as far as the eye could see. It reminded Mei of the giant wall around the INREAL GAMES studio. Back in the real world,

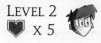

where there were no dragons and no quests. No bandits, no animal rain. She wondered for a moment if they would ever get home.

"Well, I could try shadowstepping to the other side," Rip suggested. He squeezed his eyes shut and then blinked out of view in a puff of smoke.

Half a second later he blinked back into existence, slamming headfirst into the giant doors, and falling comically onto his behind.

Rip rubbed his forehead. "So I can only shadowstep to places I can see. Good to know."

Mei chuckled and checked her spell book. "We both leveled up, so maybe I have some new spells to try. Aha!" she exclaimed.

Standing back from the doors and waving her arm in a circular motion, Mei closed her eyes and murmured a long string of words. A portal slowly appeared in front of her, and within it was a shimmering cityscape.

"After you, Ranger!" she said.

"Why thank you, Mage!" Rip replied. He did a jovial flip through the portal to the other side of the giant gates. Mei followed, and the portal closed behind them.

They were both standing on a busy street looking at a massive, bustling medieval city. Scores of tiny stalls and shops were scattered along the main road, and larger dwellings, with windows lit by lamps, skirted the city walls. Shoppers of all shapes and sizes were wandering around, haggling loudly for goods.

"Wow!" Rip said. "This is incredible! Look at all these characters!"

Frey stuck her head up out of Mei's pocket. "Urgh. The only thing worse than humans is

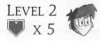

lots of humans." Her voice was still intimidating, even though she was so tiny.

"Frey, lots of these humans have sharp pointy swords," Mei warned. "And I bet they would love some of your dragon armor. So maybe you should stay out of sight, OK?"

Frey snorted in disapproval and slunk back down in Mei's pocket.

"She is the grumpiest dragon I have ever met," said Rip as they walked through the crowd. "I haven't met many, but still!"

"Hello, Dragon Riders!" a shopkeeper yelled, waving a little too enthusiastically.

Rip and Mei cautiously waved back.

"Hello, Dragon Riders!" chirped a small urchin girl, who did a quick dance in front of Rip and Mei, before scurrying off with other children in tattered clothes, skipping and giggling, in tow.

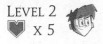

"Hello, Dragon Riders!" a blacksmith bellowed, as he bashed at what looked to be a metal sword.

"Hello, Dragon Riders!" Another shopkeeper waved with both hands at once, dropping his sandwich.

Rip turned to Mei. "Well, it seems our reputation stats did improve—everyone knows who we are!"

They continued to walk quickly through the busy shopping quarter. Mei pulled out the farmer's letter to see who it was addressed to.

> TO: Sergeant Inquisitor Darden
> CARE OF: Sillysong Inn
> MESSAGE: 'Elp! I got dem dragons eatin' all me sheep and burnin' me crops! Send 'elp!
> FROM: Farmer Jericho

Rip checked their map, and they headed straight for the Sillysong Inn.

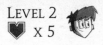

"DRAGON RIDERS!" the inn's customers called in a communal greeting as Rip and Mei stepped inside. They both waved, slightly taken aback.

Then the crowd all turned at the same time and went back to what they were doing.

The inn was full of activity. Dwarves and elves sat at tables, eating and chatting happily. In a corner on a stool sat a hooded figure sharpening a dagger. His armor was visible beneath his robe.

And at a table in the back was a group of soldiers. They all stared directly at Rip and Mei, and one of the soldiers beckoned with his finger for them to come close.

Rip and Mei cautiously made their way over to the table and sat down, aware of the guards standing around the man who had called them over.

"So, you two are the Dragon Riders, eh?"

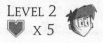

the main soldier said, his bright, shiny armor making clanking sounds as he shifted his weight.

"Yes, we are," said Mei. "Have you got a problem with that?"

"I've got a problem with you ruining my undercover bandit infiltration operation!" he said, smashing a fist onto the table. His guards immediately placed their hands on the hilts of their swords, ready for action.

"What?" Rip and Mei exclaimed, confused.

The solider pulled a coin out of his pocket and flipped it. His body seemed to shimmer and fold in on itself, and then unfold out again, revealing the short, fat bandit they had encountered earlier on the road into town. "I use this coin when I need to change my class or appearance, you interfering busybodies!"

He flipped the coin once more. His

short body folded back into the soldier again, now looking red-faced and very angry indeed.

Rip and Mei looked at each other in astonishment.

"*You're* the short, giggly little bandit who ran away?" Rip couldn't help but blurt out. A few of the guardsmen side-eyed each other and tittered, then hurriedly pretended to cough into their hands.

"What? No, I didn't . . ." the soldier blustered. "I mean, look here, you blew my operation, that's the point, OK? But I'm cutting you a break because you are the Dragon Riders," he continued. "I'm Sergeant Inquisitor Darden, how can I be of service?"

"Um, that's strangely coincidental, because we just happen to have a letter for you," Mei said, handing the farmer's note to Sergeant Darden.

He read it quickly and then tossed it over his head.

Rip's and Mei's wristbands made a trumpet

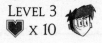

fanfare and flashed **QUEST COMPLETE**.
They were now on Level 3, with ten hearts
each!

They smiled and turned back toward
Darden.

"Farmer Jericho's problems are the least
of our problems," he said. "We have bigger
problems. The dragon war. That's a problem."

Darden didn't really have a way with
words.

Frey shifted in Mei's pocket, and Mei put
her hand up to hold her mage robe closed.

"The dragon war?" Rip asked.

"The dragon war," Darden replied. He sat
down and leaned back in his chair. The guards
all did the same. "Two factions have been
tearing this land apart for centuries. Our
land, our crops, our cities. We need you to
stop them!"

Darden pointed to a huge map that was on
the table. "Here, to the north, lies the Ice
Lands of Crystal Kingdom—the lair of the

black Lightning
Dragons that
shoot sky-magic
from their mouths!
Their leader, Lady
Nila, is a foul beast
indeed and is said
to have eaten a
thousand humans!"

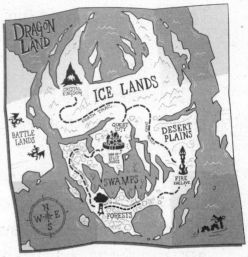

As Darden spoke,
Frey struggled even more in Mei's pocket.
Mei folded her robe more tightly around her
to quell the furious beast.

"To the south lies the territory of the Fire
Enclave," Darden continued. "Their leader is
DragonLord Garonoth. Garonoth is a
particularly ugly dragon," Darden said, and
the rest of the guards laughed.

Rip noticed tiny puffs of smoke were rising
out of a spot on Mei's robe that was starting
to glow red.

"Oh yes . . . they're all hideous beasts."

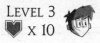

Darden spat on the floor and the rest of the guards did the same in a perfectly timed, gross ballet.

Darden continued, "In fact, if I ever come face-to-face with a dragon, I wouldn't even take its disgusting head to stick on my wall! It would be too ugly for my house!"

While the guards laughed heartily, Frey's struggles became unbearable to Mei, who now had both hands pressed firmly on her chest, barely containing the fiery green creature.

"In fact, if there was a dragon here right now," Darden said boldly, "I would call it a big, stupid, ugly tooth-head, and then strike it down with one hit of my sword!"

It was at that moment that Mei's pocket tore open. And out of it flew a very angry green dragon.

COOLDOWN'S NOT SO COOL

"**U**h . . . Mei . . . do you maybe need to recast a certain spell?!" Rip urged, staring in alarm at Frey, who was growing in size as she buzzed angrily around the sergeant's head.

"I'm trying—but it won't work!" Mei said, waving her fingers frantically to replicate the incantation.

Swatting absently at what he must have thought was a bug, Sergeant Darden stood up and glared at Rip and Mei. "Now, see here. What's all thi—"

He was drowned out by the sound of collective screams erupting in the inn as Mei's spell completely wore off.

> Where are you, nasty human soldier? I will toast you where you stand. You would insult my clan, would you? Face me, you coward!

Frey burst back into being a black-smoke-snorting, impossibly huge green dragon once more, filling the room and blocking the door.

Everyone covered their ears as Frey's voice echoed inside what was now a very

cramped space.

In spite of his earlier bravado, Sergeant Darden suddenly appeared less like a man who intended to strike down a dragon, and more like a man who was hiding under a table—as indeed he was hiding under a table, along with the other guards.

Mei was awkwardly struggling to pull her robe free from under Frey's giant foot.

A muffled sound came from ... somewhere.

Meeerrff! MEERFFF! URNGH HRRREEEER!!!

"Rip?" Mei looked around quizzically.

Frey's eyes widened and she lifted her scaly bottom slightly. The roof creaked and clouds of dust and dirt drifted down from the ceiling as she moved.

Mei heard a sudden gasp for air.

"I ... was saying, UNDER ... HERE!" Rip panted, as he slithered out from under Frey. "Gross. Now I can add 'crushed by a giant dragon butt' to my list of accomplishments." He checked his wristband. "Oh man! And I lost a heart too!"

As Frey gingerly sat back down, she glared at the surrounding scene of broken, scattered tables and terrified, quivering humans. She smiled a toothy, malevolent grin. A woman screamed and fainted.

"Back, dragon, or ... or it'll be the end of you!" Darden's wavering voice didn't sound too convincing from under the table.

"I do beg your pardon," replied Frey, not meaning it at all. "As you can see, I can't move."

She looked at Mei.

"I'm SO sorry." Mei's cheeks flushed with embarrassment. "I'm kind of new to being a mage, and I guess this spell has a cooldown on it."

"Meaning you can't cast it again until the cooldown period is up," Rip finished for Mei. "Curse it. We should have thought of that. Now what are we going to do? We're stuck in

an inn with a dragon!"

"This is your dragon?" Darden's eyes grew wider.

"I am NOBODY'S DRAGON!" Frey bellowed.

Darden cowered, retreating back under the table.

Mei interrupted hurriedly. "It's—she's really very nice, I promise you. And she currently owes us a dragon debt, so. Yay?" Mei smiled.

"She's gonna help us on our quest and everything," Rip assured Darden. Then he turned to Mei suddenly. "Mei, Frey could be the key to this whole ... dragon war ... thing. Maybe she can help us figure out a way to stop it!"

Frey's entire body shook with laughter and the inn walls trembled. "Impossible," she sneered. "The War of the Dragons has waged for eons. There is no stopping it."

"Hey," Mei said, placing her hands on her hips. "You owe us a debt, right? You don't get to choose what that debt is. Well ... we say, it's

that you help us put an end to the dragon war. Peacefully. Then you'll be released from your debt."

The entire room was in silence.

"I . . . it's impossible to . . . you can't just . . ." Frey spluttered in protest.

"We can try," Rip urged enthusiastically. "You know all there is to know about dragons. There must be a way to stop this silly feud."

Darden slowly emerged from his hiding place under the table. "If it is true, what you say, then . . . it would see an end to the destruction of farmland and homes throughout the land!"

He straightened suddenly and an exclamation mark appeared above his head. "You must travel north, to the Ice Lands. Meet with the black Lightning Dragons of Crystal Kingdom and seek peace between the clans. The fate of the land depends on you! Do you accept?"

Rip and Mei looked at each other and

replied in unison: "We accept!"

The exclamation mark above Darden's head vanished, and he nodded in approval. Thunderous applause erupted around the room as the townsfolk began to hug one another, cheer, and whoop.

"Hooray, Dragon Riders!" the crowd cheered.

"Why, this calls for a silly song—or this ain't the Sillysong Inn!" cried one woman, who righted a chair that had been toppled and climbed up onto it. She cleared her throat dramatically and sang:

> *They were called the Dragon Riders,*
> *An' they caused a great big mess.*
> *'Cos the girl, she had a secret dragon*
> *Tucked inside her dress!*
> *And the boy, he wasn't nowhere,*
> *An' he weren't havin' too much fun,*
> *'Cos when the dragon grew real large ...*
> *He got crushed under her bum!*

There was an explosion of laughter and all seemed merry once more. Rip and Mei giggled and applauded. Even Frey couldn't help a slight chuckle at the last verse of the song.

So, it was decided. The three companions would venture forth to the Crystal Kingdom to speak with Lady Nila, the leader of the Lightning Dragons. They could only hope that the black dragons would be open to the idea of negotiating with humans. And a dragon from the enemy clan.

THE CRYSTAL KINGDOM

Rip pulled the hood of his thick winter coat down hard over his face. His eyes were encrusted with snowflakes, and the icy wind chilled him to the bone. "It's so cold," he grumbled, kicking some snow with his foot.

The trio had left Quest City in good spirits. Once they were able to magically remove a wall and extricate Frey from the inn, Sergeant Darden had given them a strange coin with heads on both sides. Then they had visited town vendors to pick up warm gear.

Now they were on their main quest! If they were able to end the dragon war, there would be a massive quest reward, no doubt, and glory—maybe even a parade in their honor! But most importantly, they would be closer

to DragonLord Garonoth and his crown, which contained the precious Etherstone George spoke of.

But right now all they could do was plow on through the thick snow, making their way north to the Crystal Kingdom, lair of the black Lightning Dragons.

They had tried to ride Frey (who was NOT keen on the idea), but her wings were still too damaged from the fight with Brayden. They had all decided it was better to walk anyway. This land would be crawling with Lightning Dragons, and they'd be easily spotted in the sky.

They'd spent three long days trudging through thick snow-covered fields and icy

forests. But every time they turned a corner or took a new path, there was only more snow.

Rip stopped to rest, exhausted. He wondered if the game was cheating again, like it did back in **DIG WORLD**. But he was too cold to think any more about that now. *One foot in front of the other,* he thought. *Then sleep . . . and a campfire . . .*

Without warning, a figure slid out of the bushes directly in front of Rip. It was the mysterious robed figure from the Sillysong Inn. He had been following them! Rip opened his mouth, about to shout out to Mei and Frey somewhere up ahead, but stopped himself. The robed figure hadn't noticed him. But why? Rip was standing right out in the open.

Rip was about to reach for his bow when he saw that his hands were now

nearly transparent. He was practically invisible!

"Stealth!" Rip exclaimed out loud.

The robed figure turned suddenly toward Rip. "WHO GOES THERE!" he yelled. His hood fell back, revealing a familiar face.

"BRAYDEN?"

Rip noticed when he moved, he was no longer invisible. His stealth was now broken, and if this ability was like other video games Rip had played, he wouldn't be able to use stealth again until he was out of sight.

"Ripley! We meet again, NOOB!" Brayden replied, not lowering his axe. "Where is that stupid dragon?"

"You're not taking her scales," Rip stated. "She's our companion, and we're on a quest to stop a war."

"Why would you want to do that?" Brayden spun his axe around in his hand, smugly. "The more the dragons fight, the more quests we get to hunt them! I just need one more scale,

and I've got a full dragon armor set!" He
threw back his cloak to reveal his shiny, high-
level dragon armor, with only his chest piece
being made of slightly duller iron.

"No, Brayden. Frey is our friend. Kind of.
She's helping us, so just . . . go away!"

Rip drew his bow. A ranger class is not
built for fighting a warrior. Warriors have
too much health and armor, and Rip knew he
wouldn't stand a chance with his bow and
arrow. Plus, he didn't really want to fight
another human again, not after seeing Angela
get transformed into a massive spider in
DIG WORLD.

But Brayden wasn't giving him a choice, so
he fumbled with his bow and tried to pull out
an arrow.

Brayden examined Rip's weapon. "Nice bow;
it'll be good to add to my collection. Or to use
for firewood." He raised his shield and
charged directly at Rip.

Brayden moved faster than Rip anticipated.

He was using *charge*, a simple but familiar ability for a tank class. Rip shut his eyes and shadowstepped behind Brayden with a puff of smoke. Brayden skidded to a stop, spun about, and charged again, this time knocking Rip to the ground. Rip's wristband bleeped. Brayden had taken five of his hearts in one hit! More than half his health!

Brayden grinned menacingly at Rip, his axe raised high in the air. "Game over, NOOB!"

CRASH

A massive boulder crashed into Brayden, who went hurtling through the air, landing headfirst in a pile of snow. He was completely submerged except for his stumpy legs, which were sticking out and wriggling in the air.

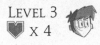

Mei was balancing on a small sheet of floating ice. She surfed toward Rip, flakes of ice and snow shooting up into the air in her wake. "Are you OK?" she asked him, already waving her arm in a circular motion, preparing for her next spell.

"I am. Took your time!" Rip grabbed his bow. "When did you learn to snow-surf?!"

"Just now! Well, I've been studying it all day. It's so much fun!" Mei did a little spin on the spot and smiled proudly. "I get new spells each time we level up! And, you're welcome. I just saved your butt!"

"Amateurs!" Brayden's tone was more annoyed than angry. He had been caught off guard, but was getting back on his feet, ready to charge at Mei.

As Mei spoke, reading from her spell book, two shackles of ice formed around Brayden's feet, locking him in place.

Mei tried to calm him down. "Brayden! Stop. We don't want to fight you!"

"Backing out of a fight because you're outmatched? That's classic Mei Lin." Brayden sneered at her. He easily pulled his legs free from the ice shackles. "Let's finish this, NOOBS. I have dragons to hunt!"

As if waiting for just the right moment to intervene, Frey burst from the trees behind Brayden, letting loose a roar of fire toward him. It was a spectacular stream of dancing flames that melted a long trail in the snow, revealing the dirt below.

Mei and Rip dived out of the way, only just in time, and Brayden barely managed to get his shield up to stop the flame from hitting him directly in the face. He fell to the ground as the huge green dragon stalked closer.

"YOU!" Frey growled, her deep voice shaking snow off the trees around them.

Brayden's eyes widened with fear as the dragon sucked in a huge gulp of air, her throat glowing red.

HEADS OR TAILS

The fire surged forth like a burning missile and if it hadn't been for Brayden's impressive armor, he would have been de-spawned for sure.

For the first time, Rip and Mei could see true terror in his eyes.

It seemed Frey's full strength was back— and now she was deadly.

"We meet again, you little metal mouse," Frey jeered, furious. "The last time we faced each other I was injured. Now I'm more of a match for you and your armor. Still fancy my scales, do you?"

"Uh ... n–no ... you can keep them," Brayden stammered. "I–I–I'm sorry!"

He began to scramble backward up the

snow-covered slope. But Frey didn't forgive so easily. With an enormous swing of her mighty tail, she knocked Brayden's shield out of his grasp. He squealed in fear, cowering before her.

Watching on in awe, Rip and Mei both snapped out of their astonished stupor.

"Uh ... Frey? I think you've made your point," Rip said, a little worried.

Frey shot him a fierce look, eyes burning ruby-red with anger. "Don't interfere, Ranger. This *tin can* and I have unfinished business."

The dragon turned her attention back to Brayden and shot another burst of flames in his direction.

"No—wait!" With his shield gone Brayden was completely exposed to the flames. In one swift movement, Mei Lin used magic to snow-surf through the flames and made a desperate grab for Brayden's hand, lifting him into the air.

At the same time Rip launched himself in a

deft, acrobatic roll toward Frey's scaly
neck, knocking the dragon off balance.
The ball of fire was sent hurtling wide
of her target.

"What is the meaning of this?!" Frey
growled, furious. "This metal-clad worm is
our enemy. Why won't you let me fight him?!"

Rip scrambled to his feet. "Because . . .
nothing is ever as simple as that, Frey. Just
let us talk to him, OK?"

Frey's eyes still glowed red with anger, but
she waited.

Rip looked around for where Brayden and
Mei had ended up, and saw them hovering in
the air, high above him, swirls of ice magically
whizzing around their feet.

"Brayden . . . I know you think this is all just
a game. But you have to believe us when we
say that something more is going on here,"
Rip called out.

Brayden shivered and looked down at
Rip intently. "Pretty smart,

fixing it so this dragon is in your party. She must be a lot higher level than you."

Mei shook her head, frustrated. "You're not listening. We have to get out of this game."

Brayden flared with anger. "Look, if you wanna leave, then leave! But this game is the coolest thing that's ever happened to me! Being one of the BETA testers? It's awesome. I didn't win that day at INREAL GAMES, but I came close—and I wanna prove to everyone that I can be the best gamer!

"At school I'm bad at everything. Like, math and science and reading and stuff. My parents get really mad. But I'm good at *this*! And if I can win this thing, well, I can show them there's stuff that I can do well!"

Mei Lin softened, suddenly seeing Brayden in a new light. It hadn't occurred to her that he might be fighting so hard to prove himself. "But why are you so mean to me at school?" she asked in a small voice.

Brayden shrugged. "I dunno. You're easy to

pick on, because you're always hanging out on your own."

Mei shook her head and scowled. "That's not an answer! And it's certainly not an excuse!"

Brayden shrugged again. He gestured toward her wristband. "You've only got one heart left. You must have caught those flames when you came through." He paused, and cleared his throat awkwardly. "Thanks, uh ... for saving me by the way."

Mei nodded a curt acknowledgment, then looked at her wristband. Brayden was right. And her robe was blackened and burned from the flames. "Oh ... that's not good."

Mei Lin floated them both back down.

"Well, geez," Rip said, "took your time."

"I'm really low on health," Mei replied, showing Rip her wristband.

"Yeah, mages are squishy," Rip said. "It's the cloth gear you're wearing. Magic's cool and all—but you're going to have to be really

careful about how much damage you take. Especially since we have no healer."

"Can't you just use a magic spell to heal yourself?" Brayden asked Mei.

Rip glared at Brayden. "No, she's a mage, dummy—not a healer. And who asked you?"

"Shut up, NOOB—it was just a suggestion!" Brayden snapped back.

"Allow me to crush him," Frey stomped forward, "and we'll be done with this nonsense!"

Suddenly, there was an enormous bellow from up in the air, and a black shadow passed over them. All four adventurers looked up. Dark, winged shapes flew by overhead. Two, no . . . three dragons. Black dragons.

"Oh no . . ." Mei quivered. "Frey's fireball . . . they must have seen it. We've given away our position!"

Brayden was visibly pale. "Three dragons? I can't fight three dragons!"

Rip's mind raced. "Maybe not . . . but *we* might be able to. As a group."

Mei pointed to her wristband. "I'll never survive this on such low health. And you're going to need magic."

Rip's shoulders slumped. "You're right . . . argh, if only we had a healer!"

Thunder clapped and the sky turned an ominous purple-black and began to crackle with lightning. A gentle snowfall that had started moments ago suddenly turned into an icy, swirling blizzard. Overhead, the Lightning Dragons were circling, watching them. The trio looked fierce. And deadly.

"The coin," Frey said, her glare still fixed on Brayden. "You can use the coin."

Mei looked up at the dragon, confused. "The coin? You mean the one Darden gave us?"

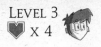

"Yes, it has the power to change you from one class to another."

"Brayden could be our healer!" Rip said, catching on.

"No way, I'm not changing into some lame healer! I'm a knight!" Brayden protested.

Mei nodded excitedly. "We would have a complete party. Healer, tank, ranger, and mage! We'd have a way better chance of winning this fight!"

"Why can't the dragon be the healer?" Brayden said sourly.

"Because Frey is a lot stronger than you, dummy," Rip jeered.

Mei shot him a discouraging look. Rip backed off.

"Frey has fire and dragon scales," Mei said against the noise of the blizzard. "She's the best chance we have at a strong defense! Please, Brayden. We don't have much time. Will you do this?"

Their faces were lit up suddenly by a sharp

crack of lightning. The three black dragons
were grouping, preparing to attack.

"HERE!" Rip threw Brayden the coin.

"How do I use it?!" Brayden shouted over
the increasingly wild wind and whirling snow.

"Toss it into the air and think of being a
healer!" Frey yelled, casting a worried glance
up into the sky.

After a moment's hesitation, Brayden
nodded and tossed the coin up high. He closed
his eyes, and his body folded in on itself in a
burst of white light.

Brayden now stood before them dressed in
a white hooded robe trimmed in gold. In his
hand was an elegant white staff, topped with
a golden sphere.

Then an earth-shattering roar bellowed
from close above, and lightning crackled all
around. The four adventurers stood with
their backs to one another in a circle,
as the menacing group of dragons
spiraled down toward them.

104

COMBINED POWER

"**O**K, NOOBS. You'd better be good at this!"

Brayden slammed his staff into the ground.

SHROOOM

A shimmering wave of green energy flew from the earth, lifting dirt and snow into the air as it went. The spell gently passed through Rip, Mei, and Frey, and the party levitated momentarily before landing, now all at full health. Even Frey's wings looked better, and she flexed them out threateningly toward the oncoming Lightning Dragons.

Brayden fell to one knee for a moment, trying to recover after casting such a big spell. Lightning crashed into the ground, missing him by inches and he stumbled

for cover, landing face-first in a pile of soft snow.

With three mighty thumps, three mean-looking black dragons landed in front of them.

Frey growled. Her whole body was glowing red, steam was snorting out of her nose in two thin jets, and she was digging her foot into the ground like a bull, ready to charge.

"Well, well, well." The biggest of the black dragons stepped forward. "Looks like we have trespassers in the Lightning Lady's kingdom. Back to destroy what's left of our lair, are you, Fire Dragon?"

As the beast spoke, flickers of lightning shot around its dark, jagged lips. Somehow these dragons looked even scarier than Frey. Their cold, yellow eyes were predatory and unmoving. Mei felt a chill crawl over her skin as they stared her down.

"We didn't destroy your precious lair!" Frey growled. She looked like she was about to explode. "It was you who were the destroyers!"

"We don't want to fight!" Mei interrupted, stepping forward. "We are here to broker peace between your factions! We wish to—"

Before Mei could finish speaking, the two smaller dragons let loose a volley of lightning from their mouths toward her. With surprising agility, Frey swung her body hard and dived in front of Mei, taking both hits on her side. Lightning sparked off Frey's scales as she absorbed the damage, wincing.

The fight was on.

Rip shot a volley of arrows at blistering speed toward the two smaller black dragons, who scattered and returned fire, lightning flying wildly.

Frey charged at the biggest dragon, digging her massive claws into the snow and flapping her big, powerful wings to gain extra momentum.

They both crashed, tumbling into the nearby trees. The smaller dragons directed their lightning attacks toward Frey, some glancing off the bigger black dragon.

"Lightning brethren! Friendly fire!" it yelled, before catching Frey's tail in the face with an almighty slap.

It was chaos. Branches sparked from lightning: The fire spread quickly and illuminated the dark sky.

Mei cast massive snotterballs at the black dragons, slowing them as they charged. The Lightning Dragons had no real teamwork and were wildly swiping their tails and firing bursts of energy at anyone in front of them.

Rip was leaping from tree to tree, disappearing into stealth when he was able and reappearing to fire off more arrows into the fray.

Brayden appeared to dance around the battle, shooting off green heals with every step.

For a moment, Mei thought he looked quite graceful, until Brayden picked his nose mid-heal and rubbed it on his robe. She screwed up her face in disgust, ducking just in time to miss a lightning bolt. It struck a tree behind her, splintering it and causing it to catch fire.

Mei cast another ice surfboard and skidded around the dragons, flinging ice balls at any she could get a clear line of sight on.

Frey was taking too much damage. The bigger dragon had managed to pin her down, while shooting lightning bolts out of its mouth. Frey deflected as many as she could with her own flames.

Just as Frey

seemed to be out of breath, a boulder of ice and goo slammed into the bigger dragon, sending it tumbling into nearby trees.

"We have to do something!" Rip shouted, narrowly avoiding a swinging black dragon tail. "They have too much Damage Per Second. If we don't act faster they'll take us down before we can control the fight!"

Mei skidded up to Rip and then snapped her fingers. "Frey, we need you!"

Frey leapt into the air and slammed back down on the ground next to Mei. She was panting hard.

"Humans, I am nearly fallen, I only have one flame burst left," she said. "But I will go down fighting these traitorous dragons until they are no more!"

"Frey, shoot your flames at us!" Mei shouted. "NOW!"

"What?!" Rip yelled, taking a step back.

"Whatever you say, human!" Frey took a long, deep breath.

"Are you crazy?!" Brayden cried, instinct causing him to hurl a flame-protective shield over the party—a spell he didn't even realize he was able to cast.

A red glow covered the team, just in time, as Frey's flames engulfed them. Rip closed his eyes tight, but the flames weren't doing damage, thanks to Brayden's spell.

The black dragons had regrouped and were now charging full speed toward them. They were laughing at the sight of them, covered in flames.

"Now, everyone, ATTACK!" Mei shouted.

The party suddenly understood. Arrows, rocks, and goo exploded out through the flames and ignited. The black dragons were caught off guard, and took the full force of the fiery volley. They stumbled and crashed to the ground.

The two smaller dragons raised their heads and howled into the night as their bodies shattered into pixels. The biggest

dragon was still standing, but wobbled as it turned its head to Frey and spoke. "We . . . will return . . . you . . . will not . . . finish . . . what YOU started!"

It collapsed to the ground, pixels scattering among the snow.

Rip's and Mei's wristbands beeped and flashed:

LEVEL 6
♥ x 20

"YES! I'm Level 8!" Brayden yelled after checking his own wristband. He triumphantly punched the air with his staff. "Brayden—one, stupid black dragons—zero! We are heroes!"

They had won. The black dragons were pixel dust.

But, standing in the circle of burning trees and loose pixels where the dragons used to be, Rip and Mei didn't feel like heroes.

INTO THE LIGHTNING LAIR

The four adventurers huddled around the fire, exhausted from a long day of fighting and walking. Frey shot another flame burst into the fire, unsettling a small swarm of firebugs hovering over the flames. They buzzed around excitedly.

Mei swatted a firebug away from her head and spoke up, cautiously. "Frey, what happened to start the dragon war?"

Frey sighed heavily. Her scales were blackened and cracked from the shocks of lightning she'd absorbed during the fight.

"That is dragon business; do not concern yourselves, humans."

"Look, Frey. I get you don't like humans. But we are in this together," Mei said. "If you tell us what happened, maybe we can help. Remember, if we can end the dragon war, your debt will be paid—you'll be free of this magical bind. Free of us."

"FINE!" Frey stood up, shaking off flakes of snow like a giant dog shaking itself dry after a swim. She began to pace, and her demeanor changed as she told her story.

"Fire and Lightning Dragons once lived in harmony. We would share responsibilities of the land. The black Lightning Dragons would use their electricity to power the cities and lights of the dragon kingdoms. We Fire Dragons would hunt and cook the food." She lowered her head. "But then on the day of the annual dragon picnic, we were betrayed. We returned home to find our Fire Enclave lair destroyed. Lightning scorched the earth,

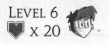

and we knew who had done it. Since then, we've been at war."

"Hang on, Frey, didn't the Lightning Dragons say *their* lair was destroyed? Was that some green dragon revenge for what they did to yours?" Mei asked.

Frey looked annoyed at the interruption, but then her expression became puzzled. "Yes, they did, didn't they? But it was ours that was destroyed. We only defended ourselves, we didn't attack their lair. They are filthy liars. Like I said, our dwellings and our food were all burned, melted by hot lava."

"Lava?" Mei shot Rip a knowing look.

"Megalava . . ." Rip said. "Megalava did this! He made you both think the other clan had destroyed your lair, and you all bought it!"

Frey snorted black smoke in anger. But then, without warning, the fire went out. Only the firebugs could be seen in the darkness. They were frenzied, making a horrible clicking noise as they buzzed about. They began to make a shape with their bug bodies.

BWAHAHAHAHAHA!
FOOLISH DRAGON, AN ALLIANCE OF THE CLANS IS IMPOSSIBLE. NILA WILL DESTROY YOU BEFORE YOU HAVE A CHANCE TO SPEAK. AND YOU . . . SILLY CHILDREN.
YOU WILL NEVER ESCAPE MY WORLD! SOON YOU WILL BE MY MINIONS FOREVER!
BWAHAHAHAHAHA!

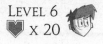

And with that, the face was gone and the campfire lit back up.

"Who—who was that?" asked Brayden.

"That was … Megalava," said Mei. "I think he's a boss, a really nasty one. One I'd rather not face. We need to get out of this world. Back to our real lives."

"Why would you want to do that?" Brayden asked. "Even with that creepy boss, this game is great! It's much better than real life."

"Because it's not a game, Brayden! You're not getting it!" Rip answered sternly. "I mean, it is a game, but it's also something much more. I don't think we can leave without the Etherstone. Plus, if we get to zero hearts, we turn into pixels and become some sort of horrible creature—minions, like Megalava said."

"Still sounds cool to me," Brayden said.

"Ugh!" Rip said in exasperation.

Mei turned to Frey. "What should we do?" she asked. "If we tell the other dragons that

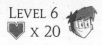

the war is Megalava's fault, they might make a truce."

"No," Frey said, "we have to go back. We can't face another battle like that. There would be many more dragons waiting in the lightning lair."

"But, Frey, you were . . . amazing," Mei said.

Rip nodded solemnly. "Like, seriously. You're leet. The leetest!"

Frey's brow furrowed. "What is . . . 'leet'?"

"It's a gamer term. It's short for elite."

Frey thought about this for a moment, and then said, "I'm just saying it's pointless to keep pursuing this foolish quest. We're all going to get electrocuted before we even get to open our mouths."

Brayden joined in. "I actually thought we were kind of boss." They all looked at him. He matched their gaze, blankly. "What? We were."

Rip shifted. "So are you, like, with us now? For good?"

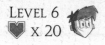

Brayden shrugged. "I guess. For now. You NOOBS obviously need me, so . . . I may as well stick around in this dumb dress and stop you guys from dying or whatever."

Mei rolled her eyes and turned to the dragon. "I know you have your reservations, Frey—but we have to see this through. There's just no other choice for us. We have to find a way out of here, and a truce is our best shot. So we're in agreement, then?"

They all looked at one another and nodded.

Frey reluctantly led the party toward their quest destination. As the last of the blizzard cleared, they could finally see through the stark, endless white. They had climbed so high the air had grown thinner and it made it more difficult to breathe. Ahead of them loomed the entrance to an

enormous cavern at the peak of the mountain. Huge crystal shards and sharp icicles jutted out from the rock, giving the effect of a huge open mouth filled with jagged teeth waiting to chomp down and swallow them whole.

They made their way through the cave's entrance, and then crept along a dark, rocky path that spiraled downward around the sparkling, crystalline walls of the cave. Peering over the path ledge, Rip and Mei could see a magnificent crystal chamber at the very bottom.

Hundreds of black dragons filled the chamber. Some were perched high on clusters of quartz. Others sat in circles playing with what looked to be very large trading cards. Some sat roasting large animals over a fire.

Rip shuddered. In the very center of the cavern's chamber, a dragon sat reclining in a large, oval-shaped basin filled with dried bones and a collection of gems, gold, and other precious items.

"That must be their leader," Rip hissed.

Frey snorted. "That's Lady Nila. She is indeed their leader. She's greedy and horrible."

"So . . . what's the plan?" Brayden whispered. "How do we get down there without them noticing us?"

Rip sighed. "There's no way we'll be able to get a word out before they start sending bolts of lightning our way. Not if that last fight is anything to go by."

Rifling through her spell book, Mei stopped at a page that said IMMOBILIZE. "This could be useful," she said excitedly, jabbing a finger at the page. "It's a spell that uses the surrounding environment to create an earthen cocoon to immobilize a target."

"That's GREAT!" Rip said. "We can use that on the dragons while we try to reason with their leader."

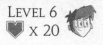 

Frey shook her head. "Their leader is fierce and very powerful. Megalava spoke truly about that—she's not just going to stand by and have a chat with you while her dragon brethren are held hostage!"

"So . . . use the spell on her too!" Rip cried.

"No good," Mei lamented. "At Level 6 I only have enough mana to cast the spell at a single target. Then, like all spells, it has a cooldown."

"Mana?" Brayden looked confused.

"Magical power," Mei explained.

Rip thought for a moment. "If only there was a way we could amplify it somehow."

Mei Lin's mind raced, taking in her surroundings. The cave's entrance, although terribly imposing, was really quite beautiful. The crystal prisms that jutted out from the rocky interior glittered pale pink and icy blue, catching the light and casting pretty reflective patterns on their faces. Mei's eyes examined the patches of dancing light, and she had a thought.

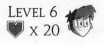

"I have an idea," Mei said slowly. "I'm not sure if it will succeed. But we'll need the element of surprise. And to act quickly and work together."

They all leaned in.

"HALT! Who goes there?" Lady Nila roared, raising her majestic head high and spreading her wings wide. She was fearsome and impressive.

Rip's Level 6 cloaking ability had engulfed them all just long enough to get them down into the heart of the dragon's crystal lair. But now the spell was beginning to shimmer and wear off. First Mei Lin appeared. Then Brayden. Then Rip. And lastly ... Frey's

enormous green form materialized into existence.

There was an instant growl and rumble throughout the room. Electricity crackled angrily in the air, and Lady Nila's eyes grew fierce as they settled on Frey.

"WHO DARES BRING THIS TRAITOR INTO OUR MIDST?!" Nila bellowed, rising to her feet, sending a litter of gems, bones, and playing cards tumbling from her nest. "DESTROY THEM!!!"

Mei wasted no time. "Brayden, NOW!" she cried.

Brayden cast a healing shield over the entire group, creating a force field of golden light to protect them. Mei raised her spell book and lifted her right arm, conjuring a vivid blue ball of light. She murmured

an incantation, but instead of directing the spell at Nila, she whirled around and launched the ball of light into the largest crystal prism she could see jutting out of the rock wall. The crystal absorbed the magical energy and magnified it, reflecting it out even stronger and brighter in multiple directions from all its faceted sides.

Ribbons of light began to fill the room. The light bounced off the many crystal shards that surrounded the chamber.

Every dragon in the chamber found itself in the path of a magical

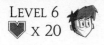

light beam, and they were all struck by the immobilization spell.

The spell caused the rocky floor to rumble and erupt. Shackles of earth and stone formed around the dragons' feet, trapping them in place. The ground continued to rise, and soon every black dragon in the lair was encased entirely in stone, with only their eyes and nostrils uncovered.

"Now, Frey," Mei Lin said urgently, lowering her arms. "The spell is only temporary. We need to be quick. It's up to you now."

Brayden's shield spell shimmered and vanished.

Frey stiffened then took a few cautious steps toward Lady Nila and cleared her throat.

"Greetings, O . . . great one," Frey said begrudgingly. Lady Nila stared furiously through her stone-statue prison, unable to reply. "We have ventured here through the snows to propose . . . an alliance. In spite of

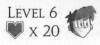

the destruction and havoc you have brought upon our homeland."

Nila's eyes burned with rage, but she was helpless against the spell. Frey continued. "The truth is, there is a greater evil than either of our great clans have faced. It has caused us to fight for so long, and so many of our brothers and sisters have been lost. We must all unite against this evil. This... Megalava."

A crack appeared in the stone encasing Nila's head, and the party all took a nervous step backward.

Frey swallowed and persevered. "I have not yet... had the blessing of the great DragonLord Garonoth. However, I feel that... that... if you... make a show of peace, he may be inclined to—"

"ENOUGH!!!" The stone encasing Nila's head crumbled away. The spell was beginning to wear off. "Enough of this senseless babbling. Do you really think we would seek peace with

you after everything your filthy clan has done? Our magnificent fortress—the work of our ancestors, destroyed!" She quivered with anger.

"Don't you see what's happening here?" Mei said urgently. "Lady Nila, the Fire Dragons' lair was also destroyed. You've been tricked! Both of you! You both had your clan's homelands destroyed—but it wasn't by either clan. It was Megalava!"

Nila's eyes narrowed. "What is a Mega... Lava?" Cracks began to ripple down the rest of her rocky form.

Rip sighed. "We're not one hundred percent sure—we think Megalava is like... the final boss or something. Only, he's not just in this land. He was in **DIG WORLD** as well. Or... at least his minions were."

"Look, we don't know anything for sure, but we do know that something evil called Megalava is behind all this and the two dragon clans fighting is just what he wants!

You have to stop!" Mei pleaded.

"I AGREE," came a booming voice from above.

Everyone looked up.

There, high up at the mouth of the cave, was DragonLord Garonoth, flanked by over one hundred green dragons, armored for battle. He was huge, with gnarled horns protruding from his scaly head. Nestled firmly between them was a crown of twisted bronze, emblazoned with a fiery jewel at its center.

"Frey, you've done well to recruit these humans, providing us with the advantage we needed to annihilate these fiends once and for all," the DragonLord sneered. "Enjoy your stone prison, Lightning traitors, for you will never see daylight again."

HOLDING ALL THE CARDS

DragonLord Garonoth slammed his massive dragon feet into the ground with an almighty clang. His dragon army circled above, fire breath lighting up the lair as they rallied and roared.

Lady Nila looked furious. The army of black Lightning Dragons were all roaring with rage within their stone cocoons, and Rip and Mei knew they wouldn't be trapped for long.

"Stop! You're all making a huge mistake!" Mei yelled.

Garonoth turned to her and growled, "This doesn't concern you anymore, human. Speak again, and it will be the last words to leave your mouth."

Rip opened his mouth to protest, but Frey

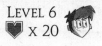

shook her head, cautioning him. "Not yet," she said, and something in her voice made Rip reconsider.

DragonLord Garonoth moved to stand directly in front of Lady Nila. The jewel in his crown shone so brightly that looking directly at it made Rip and Mei squint.

"So ... shiny ..." Brayden said, drooling a little onto his robe.

"Lady Nila, it is time to end this!" Garonoth roared into the air, and his army echoed his bellow.

"Garonoth, how typical of you to only attack when we are unable to stop you," Nila snarled. "I hereby invoke the right of Dragondecks!"

A hushed stillness fell over the lair. Both dragon clans waited in silence.

Mei turned to Frey. "What's Dragondecks?"

"An ancient battle game, played with large cards," Frey said quietly.

"A card game?" Brayden sighed loudly. "Boooring."

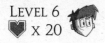

Frey continued, "It is rarely played, because it's a game of life and death. The winner gets to destroy the loser."

"OK, that isn't so boring!" Brayden said.

Garonoth circled around Lady Nila; he was enjoying the moment. "Agreed!" he said.

A giant ball of wavy, red light grew from the fiery gem in Garonoth's crown, then exploded with a shock wave that spread through the cave, shattering all the stony cocoons encasing the black dragons.

"Let the Dragondecks begin!"

Nila and Garonoth sat opposite each other. Large decks of cards hovered in front of them, held up by some unseen magic. Behind them, both armies stood, agitated at each other's presence but respecting the rules of Dragondecks.

 Garonoth, having accepted the challenge, was allowed to start first. He threw one of the large cards down onto the floor. A **PIGGOAT** materialized on top of it, with a sword and shield. It gave a loud bleat and clashed its sword against its shield threateningly.

 Garonoth pulled a new card from a pile next to him, indicating it was now Nila's turn.

"I have no idea what is going on," said Brayden. He had clearly never played a battle card game before.

 "That's a provoke card," said Rip, recognizing the character from one of INREAL GAMES' wildly successful **DRAGONDECK** series. "It has to be attacked first, before Nila can attack Garonoth directly. First one to do that wins. Now it's Nila's turn."

Brayden blinked. He wasn't getting it.

 Nila played her first card. It was a **BULLSERPENT**. She smiled

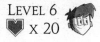
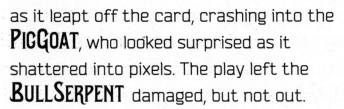

as it leapt off the card, crashing into the **PICGOAT**, who looked surprised as it shattered into pixels. The play left the **BULLSERPENT** damaged, but not out.

A cheer erupted from the black dragons, and Garonoth frowned.

Garonoth placed down two more **PICGOATS** and a **CHEESESHEEP**.

Nila followed up with five **BARRELCOWS**, who exploded onto Garonoth's cards, destroying most of his cards as well as her own. Cheese flew everywhere, with a big clump landing smack on Brayden's face. He licked his lips and said, "Mmm. Not bad."

"Nila is playing very aggressively," Mei said, watching Garonoth throw down more cards, only to be wiped away by Nila's each round. "It's a risky strategy, because the longer these rounds go on, the more chance there is that Nila will run out of cards, which will leave her open to attack."

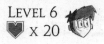
"True," Rip said to Mei, "but if she can get enough of them down quickly, she'll be able to overwhelm Garonoth before he can set up his defenses again."

"I don't get it," said Brayden.

Rip sighed, annoyed. "You won't get it until you play it yourself, Brayden. That's the only way to learn."

More rounds passed. Garonoth and Nila were visibly getting more and more distressed as their decks dwindled in size. And then it happened.

Nila was on her last card. A massive silver **ICEOGRE** appeared on the board, and promptly struck down all of Garonoth's remaining creatures in one swing.

"Oh no!" Mei said. "That's a silver! A card with direct-attack properties. Next turn it will be able to attack Garonoth directly, no matter what he puts down on the board!"

"It's over, mighty DragonLord," said Nila mockingly.

Rip and Mei noticed Garonoth did not look worried at all. He sorted through the remaining cards in his hand, and casually pulled out a shimmering gold **LavaGolem**. The black dragons gasped in unison, and the green Fire Dragons cheered.

"Oh no!" said Mei, not really knowing who she was rooting for.

Rip put his hands on his head, shocked at what was happening.

Nila was taken aback. "Where did you get that?" she cried. "That's a banned card! It's over-powered! It was removed from the decks eons ago!"

Garonoth just smiled. The **LavaGolem** let loose a fury of lava, destroying the **IceOgre** in seconds.

It was over. Garonoth had won.

"CHEATER! HACKING!" one of the Lightning Dragons called out in protest.

"Prepare yourself, Nila. It is time for DragonLord justice!" Garonoth said.

"NO!" Rip and Mei yelled together.

"Don't you see! Megalava is doing this too!" Rip shouted in frustration.

"HACKS! HACKS! HACKS!" the black dragons chanted. But they did not move to protect their leader. They could not move. Something far more powerful bound them now—DRAGONLAW. It was the same ancient magic that bound Frey in service to Rip and Mei. The Lightning Dragons were powerless against it. They could only watch on in fury and despair.

DragonLord Garonoth stepped past the **LAVAGOLEM** and stood proudly, directly in front of Nila. He breathed in deeply, his throat glowing a bright red. Nila did not close her eyes. She stared with fury and unmoving rage at Garonoth.

The mighty Fire Dragon opened his mouth to deliver the final blow.

ALL'S FAIR IN DRAGON WAR

"**C**over me!" Frey cried, and swooped down between Garonoth and Nila.

Mei panicked. "Frey, NO! We're not strong enough to protect you!" Instinctively she cast an ice shield, which popped up in a bubble around Frey.

Brayden followed suit, casting a healing shield of deflection in a bubble of gold.

Garonoth roared at Frey in fury. "INSOLENT FOOL! This is not your business! Step aside, for I will not spare you if you remain!"

Frey stood firm. "You must hear me, DragonLord! Our homeland was not—"

But she never finished her sentence.

The great inferno of flame that Garonoth had charged within him burst forth in a blaze

of searing light, engulfing the smaller green dragon. Mei's ice shield melted away almost instantly and she cried out in alarm. Brayden's shield of deflection lasted longer, but was already beginning to falter.

Rip suddenly called out, "MEI—the fruit! The magic fruit!"

Mei gasped. She retrieved the fruit and tossed it to Rip. He shadowstepped as close as he could to the flames and launched it into Frey's open mouth. She chomped down on the magical fruit in surprise.

Rip shadowstepped back to safety—though his hair and eyebrows were badly singed in the process.

Frey instantly began to glitter and glow, bright light emanating from her shining green scales. She looked down at herself in awe, for now she was engulfed in a bubble of both fire and light, seemingly unharmed.

Garonoth glared in disbelief. "What sorcery is this?!" he said, sounding a little alarmed.

The mighty DragonLord
took a small step backward.

"Lord, surely now you must
hear me. I stand before you,
risking my life to end this fight!"

Garonoth, silenced at last, nodded slowly.
"Speak, Freylaraneth. And I shall listen."

Mei, Rip, and Brayden advanced and took
their places before Lord Garonoth, though
careful not to stand too close to Frey, who
was still—impressively—on fire. Nila watched
on behind them, curious.

Frey spoke, "For generations, we have
believed that the Lightning Dragons destroyed
our home with their lightning and storm magic."
The green dragons behind Garonoth hissed in
acknowledgment and anger.

"Indeed! The evidence was clear," Garonoth
growled, "and it has taken us decades to
rebuild."

"Meanwhile," Frey continued, "the Lightning
Dragons had their home destroyed by fire."

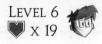

The black dragons erupted into roars of anger.

"It's true, we returned from a hunt to find nothing remained of our lair but ashes," Nila spoke, sadness in her eyes. "There was … a nest. With eggs …" Her voice trailed off, stricken with grief.

Garonoth's scaly brow furrowed. "We were responsible for no such attack."

Nila stepped forward and matched Garonoth's gaze evenly. "And neither were we."

"Then … then who?!" the DragonLord spluttered.

Mei spoke up, waving a hand to draw attention to herself. Boy, did she feel tiny. "We believe there is a great evil plaguing this land— and many others. He is known as Megalava."

"And he has minions," Rip added. "My lord … can I ask … where did you get that playing card? The one you used to win the Dragondecks battle?"

Garonoth stiffened. "**LAVAGOLEM** … yes, it

was... a gift. It was left at the gates of our kingdom encased in a chest of volcanic rock. We know not where it came from. Though, I seem to recall some strange insects buzzing about when we opened the box."

"Firebugs," said George from right beside them, speaking up as if he had been there the entire time.

"ARGHH!!" Brayden leapt high into the air in surprise. "What the—where did you come from?!"

George looked around confused. "Me? Oh, I don't know, really. Where do any of us come from?"

"He does that a lot," Rip said dryly.

"The point is," George continued, "the insects you saw were firebugs. They are Megalava's spies."

Garonoth's eyes widened and he snorted with anger. "Spies?! In my kingdom? Explain yourself, Wizard."

"Well, I could—but I'm afraid we don't have much time. You see, there's an army of Megalava's minions on their way here. RIGHT NOW. You two giant lizards were supposed to destroy each other. But now you know the truth. So I imagine you aren't going to do that anymore. Am I correct?"

Garonoth and Nila looked at each other in mutual understanding for the first time.

"If what these creatures say is true, I bear no more ill will against you and your clan, Nila," said Garonoth solemnly.

"Nor I you," Nila replied, allowing herself a toothy smile. She projected her voice for all to hear. "DragonLord Garonoth! Could this truly mean peace between us, after all these—"

"NO TIME!!" George interrupted loudly, banging his staff on the cave floor. "Megalava's army of nasties will be here to finish the job you failed to do. Only they'll want to finish us all!"

MELTING POT

With a crack so loud that Rip, Mei, and Brayden had to cover their ears, the crystal walls of the Lightning Dragons' lair began to shatter. Long spikes fell from the upper walls, crashing dangerously into the ground, and revealing a red sky above. Frey threw her wings protectively over the gamers.

Dragons, green and black, scattered for cover.

"How is this happening?" yelled Garonoth.

"The game must be cheating!" Rip shouted.

"To the sky! Quickly now! Zoom, zoom!"

called George. He hopped onto his staff like it was a broomstick and took off.

"GET ON, HUMANS!" Frey shouted, and Rip and Mei climbed aboard her scaly back.

"I am NOT getting on that thing. I hate flying!" Brayden stamped his foot like a spoiled child.

DragonLord Garonoth grabbed Brayden as if he were a toy doll and threw him over his back. Before Brayden could protest, the mighty horned dragon leapt into the air, ice bouncing off his large wings as they slowly flapped, gaining altitude.

Nila and Frey followed, and all three dragons soared high into the mess of tumbling rock and ice above. Mei shot a glance back at the lair, only to see it bubble into a red mess of lava. A few moments more and they would have melted.

The two dragon armies flew fast and regrouped in the air, each with their leader at the front.

"What's that?" Mei said to Rip, pointing ahead.

A massive red cloud was moving toward them. But it was moving too fast to be a cloud.

"FIREBUGS!" yelled Rip.

They hit the firebug cloud with surprising force. Each bug felt like being struck by a fast moving bottle cap. Frey was taking the brunt of the swarm, but she was having difficulty maintaining her speed as more and more bugs landed and clung to her body.

Rip and Mei tried to swat them away, but it was hard to do that and hold on to Frey at the same time. Plus, the firebugs were quite sharp and hot to touch.

"Do a barrel roll!" Rip and Mei yelled together.

Frey obliged, pulling in her wings and spinning like a corkscrew. The firebugs scattered in all directions, detaching as Frey plowed through the swarm and out into the clear air. She hovered for a moment, looking around for the rest of the armies, but they were still lost in the firebug cloud behind them.

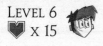 
"What now?" asked Rip.

"I don't know," replied Mei, shaking a few stowaway firebugs from her hair.

"I DO," said a sharp, high-pitched voice.

And there, directly in front of them, was the boss. It had two long wings, flapping so fast they could barely be seen, which created a strange mechanical humming sound.

The creature's huge bug eyes were similar to that of a fly, and its head twitched left and right randomly as it hovered. It was about as big as Frey, but with the long body of a praying mantis. It had two dangerous-looking claws, and a long red stinger that wagged like a dog's tail behind it. The entire creature looked like it was made of metal and cogs.

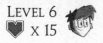
"So. These are the Dragon Riders I keep hearing about," it chirped. "You don't look very important. I don't know why I have to bother with you."

Frey cocked her head slightly, confused by what she was looking at. "You don't belong here," she said coldly. "You are . . . different."

"Be quiet, little sprite," the creature said dismissively, "or I will call Megalava to come down here and delete you permanently."

Frey growled, but did not move.

"Who are you?" asked Mei. "What do you want?"

"Who am I? I am Megamantis. A high-minion of Megalava," the bug chirped proudly. "What do I want? I want to go home. This world reeks of humanity. Dirty organics in our code. Unpredictable. Disorganized. Smelly."

The creature looked at Rip and Mei with disgust. It really did not seem to like humans. Maybe even more than it disliked Frey.

"It doesn't matter, little pests. Soon you'll
be a part of the code. A part of the machine.
You two have been kicking up quite a ruckus,
you see. Most adventurers don't make it this
far, but you just keep on surviving." Its
stinger flicked back and forth, seemingly
excited about the thought of a fight.

"You don't scare us!" said Rip defiantly.
"Boss fights are kind of our speciality."

"Yes, but have you ever been in one where
your life depends on it?" Megamantis asked,
one of its arms rubbing over its eye, like a
cat cleaning its face.

This caught Rip and Mei off guard. This
creature knew about the game—it spoke
of code and deleting. It confirmed their
worst fear: that losing a battle in-game
really did mean being trapped forever. If
that happened, they'd never see their
families again. They'd have to live out their
lives as horrible minion creatures . . . like
Angela . . .

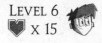

Megamantis clapped its insectoid hands together. "Enough chat, prepare to—"

Before it could finish its sentence, Frey charged forward, howling blasts of fire breath wildly.

Mei conjured an ice surfboard and began shooting a combination of rock balls, snot balls, and ice balls at Megamantis. The bug dodged her fire with ease.

Rip stood up on Frey's back and unleashed a volley of arrows. Again, the creature darted about in the sky, avoiding most of the damage.

Mei then realized the creature wasn't attacking. It was toying with them. Analyzing their moves and attack patterns with its huge bug eyes.

Frey went in for another pass, fire hurling out of her wide mouth. She was really going for it. Then Mei saw something in the creature's stance change.

"Wait, Frey!" she yelled, but it was too late.

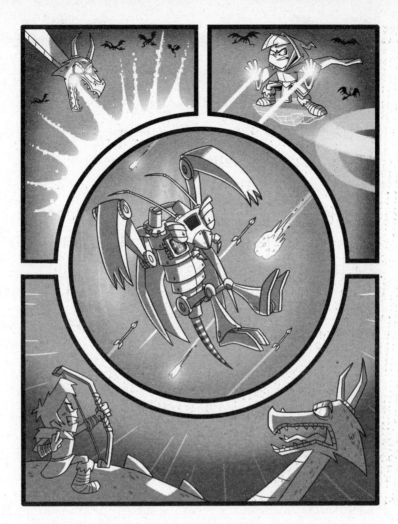

Frey was charging for a second frontal
assault. Megamantis remained still, until Frey
was only a few feet in front. Then it
sidestepped, and plunged its huge red stinger
into Frey's side. The stinger snapped off, still

deep in the mighty dragon. Pixels flew from the hit, and Frey's flapping grew sluggish as red veins started to spread from the stinger's impact point.

"No!" cried Mei, as she surfed over to Frey and Rip.

Frey was starting to spin and was losing altitude quickly. Then more quickly. Then she was simply falling straight down.

"Rip ..." Frey called, using his name for the first time. "Let go, Rip."

"Hold on, Frey, I can get it out!" Rip said, desperately trying to reach the stinger.

Mei pulled up beside them, matching their speed in the dive, as the ground got closer.

"Take him, Mei ..." Frey said with a strained but loud voice, and she did a barrel roll. Rip flew off into the air and Mei grabbed him, managing to pull up just in time, as Frey crashed into a large clearing below.

Mei angled her surfboard in a wide arc, with Rip holding on to her, and glided over to

where Frey had crashed. They stepped off
the surfboard and ran to her.

"Frey!" yelled Mei, trying to pull out the
stinger.

Frey was starting to shimmer. She lowered
her head, looking at Rip and Mei with her
ancient dragon eyes. "The war is ended; my
debt to you is paid. You two truly are Dragon
Riders."

Frey shimmered one more time and then
shattered into thousands of pixels. Rip and
Mei stood silently over her. Pixels fell from
Mei's hands where the stinger had been.

Their friend was gone.

QUEST COMPLETE

"Oh, very touching," came a voice from behind them. Rip and Mei spun around to see Megamantis sitting on a rock, smiling and clapping. "No need to weep! She was just a sprite. A bit of code. A Non-Player Character."

"She wasn't just an NPC!" Mei shouted, wiping a tear from her face. "She was our friend!"

"You'll pay for this!" Rip said. "We'll put an end to you!" He quickly launched a volley of arrows, but they only bounced off Megamantis's metallic skin.

Megamantis smirked. "Yeah? You and what army?"

"That one!" Mei pointed to the sky.

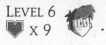

Corkscrewing through the distant firebug cloud were hundreds of black and green dragons, flying together in perfect triangular formation.

Nila, Garonoth, and George were at the front. Brayden was still clinging to Garonoth's back, and not having a good time.

"Actually, TWO armies!" said Rip.

Megamantis opened its mouth wide in shock and spread its wings, ready to flee.

Mei cast a continuous blast of ice at the creature's feet, locking it into place. "You're not going anywhere!" she said.

Rip shadowstepped and reappeared behind Megamantis, shooting bolas arrows at the creature's wings to slow their flapping.

"Now, dragons, FIRE! Everything you have!" yelled George. "Pew! Pew!"

A giant column of lightning and fire lit up the sky, hitting Megamantis with such force that the ground raised up above them all and collapsed back down in a mini earthquake.

The air was so thick
with smoke, fire, and
static electricity, Rip
and Mei could taste it.

Slowly, the dirt settled
and the smoke cleared.
Megamantis was on one knee.

One side of the creature was now mostly
pixels, the other half somehow managing to
survive the attack. This was one tough boss.

"Cheaters! Hacks!" Megamantis yelled.

It punched a strange marking on its chest
with its arm and, in a whirl of white pixels,
disappeared. The remaining firebugs sparkled
with red fire, before they too scattered and
vanished.

It was over. They had won.

"Back, fiends, to the volcanic fires of filth
you came from!" Nila roared triumphantly,
wings flapping as she soared through the air.

Garonoth took a place beside her and gave
her a nod of respect.

"From one leader to another: You and your clan fought bravely, Nila." Garonoth's rumbling voice was loud enough for every dragon in the sky to hear.

Nila bowed her head in gratitude.

"Yeah, totally, guys. You kicked some serious lava butt!" Brayden chimed in, giving Lord Garonoth a congratulatory pat on his shiny green back.

The DragonLord snorted a plume of smoke in disapproval. "Your friends are waiting." Garonoth banked toward where Rip and Mei were standing, dirty and battle-worn. Both dragons touched down effortlessly, and Brayden gratefully leapt to the ground.

"Ohhh, sweet, precious, awesome LAND!" he said, laying himself flat, facedown, and awkwardly hugging the earth. He stood up, dusting himself off, then asked, "Hey, where's Frey?"

Rip shook his head. "She didn't make it, Brayden."

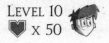
"She died. Fighting for us," Mei whispered. "Frey's ... a hero." She couldn't stop the tears that spilled down her cheeks. Rip put a hand on Mei's shoulder, and blinked back tears himself. It had all happened so quickly. Frey was their friend. It wasn't fair.

Garonoth looked solemnly to the sky. "She was a courageous fighter. They will sing songs of her bravery for years to come." He let out a mighty roar in tribute. From the sky, hundreds of dragons could be heard echoing the call as a mark of respect.

"Wait!" Brayden looked down at his hands. "Can I do something? I'm the healer, right?"

Nila lowered her head to look more closely at the human adventurers. "Is that possible?" she asked.

"Not if she's already ... already ..." Mei struggled to finish her sentence.

"DEAD?" George said, miraculously popping out of thin air, as usual. They all jumped, startled.

"Would you STOP DOING THAT?" Rip growled, in no mood for George's silliness. They'd just lost a friend!

"My dear, cotton-ball-headed heroes!" George sang, skipping around them in a circle. "You completed a boss battle! The experience you gained from that fight was astronomical! Check your levels!"

Rip, Mei, and Brayden obeyed, examining their wristbands.

Mei gaped. "Mine says Level 10!"

"Mine too!" Rip replied, stunned. "And we've got fifty hearts!"

"WHOA. Dudes. I'm Level 12!" Brayden whooped.

George nodded enthusiastically. "You've had the power of resurrection since Level 11."

A smile slowly spread across Rip's face. "Res . . . resurrec—you can bring Frey back to life, Brayden!!"

Brayden smiled. "Oh . . . cool, man. So, do I just cast it? Right here?"

George nodded and they all held their breath.

Brayden pulled back the sleeves of his shiny white robe, shutting his eyes tightly. A great white circle of light appeared and everyone took several steps back to make room for it as it grew.

Strange symbols appeared in the earth, branded in light and fire as the glow grew larger and brighter. There was a great flash, and the entire party had to shield their eyes from its brilliance.

As the magic diminished, Rip, Mei, Brayden, George, and the dragons all tentatively opened their eyes.

THE PARTY

The entrance to the Fire Enclave's lair was through a giant dragon's head, impressively carved into a cliff face in the middle of the desert.

Merriment was in the air as dragons from both clans ate, sang, and danced together for the first time in generations. Rip and Mei had no idea that dragons loved to sing, and now with the celebrations in full swing inside the Fire Enclave's lair, they were getting the full set list.

Some songs were better than others. Mei didn't quite like the ones about farts, and there were a lot of those songs in particular. The worst was "A Fart to Remember," which was a long song about an ancient dragon who

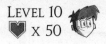

fell in love with a fart, and they eventually got married and had stinky children.

Mei thought it didn't make much sense, but Rip and Brayden had seemed to thoroughly enjoy it.

The celebration hall was enormous. There was one long clay table laden with enormous, dragon-sized portions of food. Giant chairs lined either side, and Frey and the three gamers were seated close to Lady Nila and Lord Garonoth at the head of the table. George had disappeared again.

Frey had received a medal for bravery, which she proudly wore around her neck. Brayden had stood awkwardly while he was sung a song of praise by the Dragon Priests

for his superb healing. He had picked his nose throughout the entire melody.

The townsfolk of Quest City had been invited to the celebration, and a few of them had already needed first aid after being sat on by some especially large dragons. Most of the still-healthy townsfolk and dragons were watching Sergeant Darden and his guards (the "Darden Dancers"), who were dressed in ceremonial purple armor and performing an incredibly complicated dance routine.

"Great hustle, knights!" Darden cried as he and his crew took a break to sit with Brayden, Rip, and Mei. "Dragon Riders, well done on completing your main quest!"

"Thanks, Sergeant Darden!" said Rip. "It's easily one of the best quests I have ever been on."

"Yeah!" Mei added. "Except for the cheating by Megalava."

Darden sighed. "Ah yes. Megalava and his minions."

"You *knew* about Megalava?" Rip asked.

"Oh yes," Darden replied. "It seems like every time an adventurer appears to be doing well, one of Megalava's minions turns up and puts a stop to them. Not you three though! Well done! Our city is now safe, and—"

"Reward please," interrupted Brayden. "Skip the story, thanks."

Rip and Mei shot him annoyed looks. They never skipped the story. When it came to role-playing games, the story and getting lost in the lore of the world was half the fun. Obviously Brayden was just after loot and nothing else.

"Very well," said Sergeant Darden. With a click of his fingers his guards lifted a huge golden chest onto the table. "This is yours, Brayden."

A bright golden light poured out of the chest as Brayden slowly lifted the lid. He

pulled out a variety of weapons, spell books, and a huge bag of gold coins.

"Sick," Brayden said, as he held all the loot in his arms and stood up from the table. "OK, I'm bored of this game now. What's next?"

Darden stood up and shrugged. "To be honest, I'm not really sure what you all should do next. No one has ever completed the main quest before!"

Ripley, Mei, and Brayden looked at one another, worried. How many BETA testers had come into this world and never made it out?

Ten? Twenty? A thousand?

Darden clicked his fingers again. "Come on, dancers! Our fans await!" He stood up, and the Darden Dancers all twirled back onto the dance floor.

"So, we just . . . stay here?" Brayden asked. "I don't want to stay here. I've beaten the main quest. I've got all the loot—and you can't have any of it, by the way. I'm done with this game now."

"Hang on a second," Rip said, remembering. "George told us to find something. A rock?"

"**ThE EThERSTONE!**" Mei exclaimed. "He said it was our way out of this world!"

"What's the Etherstone?" Brayden asked.

Mei pointed at Lord Garonoth. "He's wearing it."

"So . . . how should we do this?" Rip asked, nibbling gingerly on some meat attached to a bone that was almost too heavy to lift off the table.

Mei fidgeted nervously. "I think we should just be up-front and ask."

Rip nodded slowly, chewing. "OK." He swallowed. "Why don't you do the talking."

Mei rolled her eyes and stood, leaving her own enormous charred meal untouched. Rip followed.

Lord Garonoth tossed the bone he'd been using to pick his teeth over his shoulder and gazed down at the two adventurers as they approached.

"Dragon Riders is what they call you, isn't it?" He lifted a scaly eyebrow.

Mei Lin nodded and started to explain. "When we first, er, fell into this world, we landed on Frey's back. It was ... all just a misunderstanding, really. But the name stuck."

"Yeah," Rip chimed in, "and it turns out riding dragons is *awesome*!"

Mei shot him a look. "I thought you were going to let me do the talking!" she whispered.

Rip cleared his throat, motioning for her to continue.

"Lord Garonoth, we have been traveling throughout this land on a great quest. We have faced many dangers. Fought many enemies. But we have triumphed in our goal to bring the two dragon clans together—and peace to the land!"

Garonoth nodded slowly. "I see. And now you are looking for some kind of reward, is that it?"

Mei Lin swallowed. "We . . . we really wouldn't ask. Usually. It's just . . . we're trying to get home. We're not from here. And we believe . . . you have the item we need to leave this place . . ."

Garonoth's eyes widened curiously. "Oh? What on earth could I possibly have that you two tiny humans need?"

Mei hesitated. Then Rip pointed to the crown on the DragonLord's head.

Suddenly, all the noise and songs and dancing in the room came to an abrupt halt. Someone gasped dramatically.

Garonoth simply held their gaze. The moment seemed to stretch for an eternity. "You cannot mean my crown," he said, his voice terrifyingly quiet.

"Er, no!" Mei said hurriedly. "Well, not exactly. Just that shiny jewel. In the center of the crown."

Garonoth raised a clawed hand up to the crown and delicately removed it from his head, gazing at it thoughtfully.

"This crown has been in my family for generations. The leader of the Fire Dragons has always worn it as a display of power."

"Yes, but it's only the jewel we need," Mei said, her voice faltering.

"And we did unite the dragon clans! Surely we've earned some kind of reward!" Rip added.

Garonoth considered this for a moment longer, before offering a curt nod. "Very well!" he boomed loudly. "Let it be known, that as fair and just reward for uniting the warring dragon clans and bringing peace to the land, I shall bestow upon these two heroes the ancient sigil!"

The dining hall of the Fire Enclave erupted in thunderous applause and cheering, and the music and dancing resumed once more.

Rip and Mei looked confused.

"Sigil?" Rip wondered curiously. "I thought it was a jewel."

Mei shrugged.

Garonoth plucked the gemstone from its setting in the crown, and immediately its brilliant shine dimmed. The DragonLord leaned down before the two heroes and unfurled his claws to reveal the Etherstone.

Rip and Mei both gasped.

It was not a jewel at all.

"Another medallion!" Rip exclaimed.

"I don't believe it!" Mei stared in amazement.

The medallion was identical in size and shape to the one they'd found in **DIG WORLD**. But this one had the shape of a dragon with outstretched wings carved into the center.

They both reached into the dragon's palm and took the medallion, thanking him, and examined the prize between them.

"Use it wisely. There's powerful magic in that sigil," Garonoth warned.

"Trust us, we know," Rip said.

Suddenly, there was a commotion on the dance floor. Among the whirling and dancing

dragons, George the Wizard could be seen waving his staff angrily. "Watch where you're stepping, you great lizard oafs!" he wailed.

George spotted Rip and Mei and skipped over to them. "Ah! There you all are!" he exclaimed, offering a hurried bow to DragonLord Garonoth.

"George!" Mei Lin grabbed him by the shoulders. "Care to explain this?"

Rip held up the medallion. "How many of these things are there?" he asked desperately.

Both he and Mei looked weary and exasperated. George studied the two adventurers, as if deciding something.

"Perhaps it's time I told you both the truth," he said, seriously. It was odd, he seemed to change for a moment—as if he were someone else entirely, not a wacky wizard. "Meet me in the Dune Tower."

And with that, he was gone.

CLANS UNITED

The Dune Tower was an impressive sandstone structure that stood at the very top of the Fire Enclave. The room at the top was large enough for a number of dragons to sit. In the center was a circular fire pit, burning with low, hot coals.

When Rip and Mei arrived, George was waiting for them, gazing out across the desert. "When I built this area, I remember

thinking this tower was beautiful. But it truly is breathtaking, seeing the whole landscape from here," he murmured.

"You helped the dragons build their lair?" Rip asked.

George chuckled. "Yes, in a way. But I didn't use sand. Or even magic." He turned to face them. "I used code. Just like I did when I created **DIG WORLD**."

Rip and Mei both froze.

"What... what are you saying?" Mei stammered. "You're the game designer?!"

George nodded and smiled sadly. "I'm afraid so. Well, I'm one of the developers at INREAL GAMES.

"But I was the best! This game was my idea! Lots of games within the one major game. With levels of every genre—survival, fantasy, space..."

Mei gaped in awe. "So just how many levels are there in this game?!"

George scratched his head. "I—I don't remember. Everything gets foggier the longer I'm stuck here."

Rip and Mei exchanged looks of despair. "So that's how you're able to pop in and out the way you do. But... you're stuck in the game too?"

George nodded. "'Fraid so. I still have a few tricks up my sleeve, though. Like getting you two in here to beat it! You got my package—my specially modified BETA console. And because of that, you two are the only ones with a real chance of beating the game!"

Rip found himself getting very, very angry.

"YOU sent us the console?! It's because of YOU that we're stuck in here?!" Rip's voice was loud and shrill.

"But how did you send us a package in the real world . . . if you're stuck inside the game?" Mei asked.

George looked mischievous. "I have my ways. Systems I can still infiltrate from within, as long as there is an internet connection. Which, of course, there always is, because everything is online now! I can hack the postal system from within this mainframe. Manipulate the code."

Rip shook his head in frustration. "But why us? We lost the competition that day at INREAL. Everyone else scored way higher than we did."

George nodded. "Indeed they did. But I was watching you. I saw everything. In spite of the silly mistakes you made in getting caught up competing against each other, I'd never

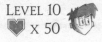 

seen such talent! You were both magnificent! I knew that if anyone had any hope of beating this, it would be you two!"

"How did you get stuck in here in the first place?" Mei Lin asked.

George's brow furrowed and he looked almost pained. "You know ... I–I don't entirely remember. But around the time I finished creating all the various levels and genres in the game, I began to code the 'enemy.' You know, the evil thing you need to defeat in order to win the game. I made him fearsome! Gave him minions in every level. It was some of my finest work!"

George paused, as though trying hard to remember. "But something went wrong when I created the virtual reality component. There was a glitch in the code. One day, I put on the VR headset to test the final level and ... I died. The enemy I had created, Megalava, was too strong. Too powerful. I'd made the game much too hard. And instead

of just re-spawning like I'd designed, I didn't go anywhere. I was stuck inside the game!"

"Couldn't one of the other developers help you? You know, from the outside?" Mei Lin asked.

"Believe me, they tried. But nothing worked! Others have disappeared too."

"Oh, great," Rip said sarcastically. "So you gave the game to a bunch of kids next."

George smiled apologetically. "I understand it may seem a bit harsh . . . but, you see, you kids are such amazing gamers, you're capable of things adults aren't. To be frank—you're better gamers than we are."

Mei sniffed haughtily. "That much is true."

"So that's why we're here," Rip said. "To beat the game and get you out."

"Not just me," George said solemnly. "Anyone who dies in this game is stuck in here. Which is why it's EXTREMELY IMPORTANT that neither of you die! You're the last chance any of us have of getting out!"

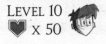

Mei shook her head. "But, how are we supposed to beat the game, George? You said yourself, you made Megalava too tough. And now he's all . . . glitched out and messing with the rules!"

"The medallions," George said excitedly. "The medallions were my fail-safe. I coded a portal key to crash out of the program from any level in the game. But when I faced Megalava, the key was broken and the fragments were split over every level in the game. I know where some of them are, but not all. What I do know is that you have to find every single medallion to get everyone out alive."

"I see. Once we have all the medallions, we can join them together to re-form the portal key and get everyone out!" Mei said, growing excited.

"So there's still hope for Angela!" Rip said, remembering their classmate, still stuck in **DIG WORLD** in the form of a spider.

"There's hope for us all—as long as you two

keep gaming!" George exclaimed. "I know you can do this."

Rip and Mei looked at each other.

"Well, I guess we don't have a choice," Mei said with a sigh, pulling out the medallion with the dragon on it. "All right, so what's the next game?"

George shrugged. "Don't remember."

"What?! But you designed it!" Rip cried.

"I told you, I'm all foggy!" George said, tapping his head. "But whatever it is, you'll both do marvelously, I'm sure! Let's get this show on the road. Now, what we need are those two dragons."

George snapped his fingers, and in an instant Lord Garonoth and Lady Nila appeared, looking very confused.

"How did we get to Dune Tower?" Garonoth growled, looking around.

"Never mind that now," George said. "I need you to perform one final task, as a display of peace!" He motioned to the fire pit. "Fire and

lightning united! This act shall seal the pact of peace!"

Nila nodded. "If it is what must be done, then I see no harm in it."

Garonoth agreed. "Very well. But this nonsense ends after we do this. I've had enough of you meddling humans!"

Lord Garonoth and Lady Nila took their places opposite the fire pit. In unison, they unleashed a mighty burst of fire and lightning into the fire pit. The two forces combined to form a magical ball of energy that crackled and turned a brilliant white.

Rip and Mei both recognized it instantly. It was the exit portal.

"You see! That's why the dragon clans had to be united!" George clapped excitedly. "Not only to bring peace to the kingdom, but because it was your ticket out of here! Am I a good game designer, or what?!"

"We have to say good-bye to Frey!" Mei said.

Rip nodded. "Do you think you could 'magic' her here? And Brayden as well?"

George smiled and snapped his fingers. Frey blinked into view. Alongside her was Brayden, who was clutching an enormous half-chewed bone against his belly. "Urgh . . . meat sweats," he groaned. "I'm never eating again!"

Frey glanced about, taking in the portal and then Rip and Mei. "I suppose you're leaving," she said softly.

Rip and Mei raced over to their dragon friend and threw their arms around her shiny green neck.

"I wish we didn't have to leave you. But we

have an even bigger quest to complete. In a different land." Mei pressed her face against the smooth, warm scales she'd become so familiar with.

Frey smiled. "You are the finest heroes I've ever met." She smiled. "And the stinkiest."

"Come, now," George urged, "untold adventure awaits!" He gestured them toward the portal.

Brayden wandered over to the globe of bright, white light. "Is this how we log out?"

Rip slapped a hand on his shoulder. "Not exactly," he smiled wryly. "We're not going to be able to do that for a while. Come on, we'll explain on the way."

"WAIT A MINUTE!" George cried. "He can't go with you." He waggled a finger at Brayden.

"What? What do you mean?" Brayden's eyes widened.

Mei stepped forward. "George, don't be silly. He brought Frey back to life! He's with us now!"

Rip nodded fiercely. "Yeah, we can't just leave him behind."

George shrugged. "Well, I'm afraid you'll have to. You are the only ones playing the game through the console I modified. So the medallion pieces will work as a portal for the two of you alone. Your friend simply cannot pass through, even if he tried."

Panicking, Brayden pushed past George and shoved both hands toward the portal's swirling surface. The portal instantly became firm to his touch, like glass.

"NO! This isn't fair!" Brayden whirled around, his voice cracking.

"George, can't you just re-hack Brayden's

console to let him through as well?" Rip
ventured.

George's shoulders slumped. "Sadly, no.
Modifying yours was the only chance I had.
And this portal won't last forever, either.
You'd better get a move on. Your friend will
be fine here. This world is still full of quests
to keep him occupied. I should know, I
designed them all!"

Rip turned to Brayden and winced.
"Brayden...I..."

Brayden's expression darkened. "No, I get it.
Really. You guys only wanted my help when
you were in a bind, but now you're just going
to leave me behind like garbage! Some *heroes*
you are. I can't believe I actually thought..."
He folded his arms angrily and turned away,
trying not to let his face betray how hurt he
really was.

Mei's eyes pricked with tears. "We will
come back for you as soon as we fix this mess,
I promise! Please, Brayden, you have to—"

"NO TIME!" George yelled, pointing at the portal, which was beginning to shimmer and fade.

"Mei, we have to go, NOW!" Rip grabbed her hand and pulled her toward the magical exit.

"Stay safe, Brayden. We will come b—"

But Mei never finished her sentence.

LOADING...

Rip! We're back in the loading screen. Look, the other medallion is still there.

I guess this new medallion goes here . . .

LEVEL TWO: DRAGON LAND COMPLETE! ENTERING LEVEL THREE!

Mei Lin's eyes slowly opened and she was faced with a fluttering checkerboard of black and white. Something heavy was on her head.

A helmet?

Suddenly, she heard a loud beeping sound, kind of like a horn.

BEEEEEEEEP!!

The checkerboard flapped out of view, and Mei realized it was a flag. Looking down, she saw she was seated in a vehicle of some kind.

Another blast of a horn.

BEEEEEEEEP!

There was a sudden roar of engines growling to life around her. Mei looked at herself. She was no longer clad in the delicate